In the Line of Fire

"You've got a bad enemy coming around who thinks you don't belong on your land," Jeremy said.

"Yes," McAdam said. "And it makes me worried about having you live here with me."

"Oh, I see. As soon as you get angry with me, then everything is off!"

"But I'm not angry with you. Jeremy, you misunderstand—"

"Yeah, sure I do."

"No, I mean it," said McAdam, moving in closer.

"Take your hand off my shoulder!"

But just as Jeremy ducked away, the rapid crackle of bullets jolted them both. "Down!" McAdam screamed. He pushed the boy to the ground and threw himself on top of him.

HUNTED!

HUNTED!

LARRY WEINBERG

Rainbow Bridge
Troll

Copyright © 1995 by Larry Weinberg.
Cover illustration copyright © 1995 by Troll Communications L.L.C.

Published by Rainbow Bridge, and imprint and trademark of Troll Communications L.L.C.

Cover design by Tony Greco & Associates. Cover illustration by Kersti Frigell.

Printed in the United States of America.

10 9 8 7 6 5 4 3 2 1

With gratitude to Joanne Mattern, my editor,
who worked on and for this book
almost as hard as I.

CHAPTER

The heavy iron lid of the big garbage bin behind the supermarket was rising on its hinges, as if by itself. First came the smell of rotting vegetables, then of a turkey that would never make it as far as anybody's oven. Finally, the head of a boy poked up, warily turning this way and that as he peered into the gathering darkness.

For a brief moment his gaze rested suspiciously on the man sitting inside a pickup parked at the rear of another store about twenty feet away. But the fellow was slumped over the wheel, as if napping, and Jeremy couldn't stand hiding inside that Dumpster any longer.

Vaulting over the side, he landed in a crouch. The man stirred, but the boy had already exploded like a sprinter for the twelve-foot-high wire fence that ran behind the Black Mountain Shopping Center as a protection against rockslides.

He took a flying leap at it. As soon as his thin fingers

seized hold of the mesh, his sneakers dug in and he began to climb like a squirrel. He didn't see the man in the truck scratching at his white beard and wondering where this boy could possibly be going. Beyond the fence was nothing but brush stretching into deep woods. And rising up steeply behind that was only the thick and towering darkness of the mountain.

Suddenly, there was a spill of revolving colored light. Jeremy turned. A patrol car was just nosing its way through the little alley that ran between the side of the supermarket and a gun store. The boy glanced up. Too far to climb without being seen!

But the pickup had already jolted into motion. He caught a glimpse of the driver signaling for him to drop down into the back of the truck as it swerved to a stop just beneath him. There was no time to hesitate—the patrol car's windshield was coming into view, the officer inside already starting to turn the wheel this way.

Jeremy let go and fell to his knees against the bulging tarp. He clawed at it until he'd pulled up an edge, then dove underneath. There was only enough time to hunker down between two large sacks before the patrol car pulled up beside the truck and both engines shut off.

Jeremy heard windows being rolled down. Then the man in the truck said calmly, "Evening, Deputy Tippet."

"Do I know you?"

"I think so. I'm that big pain in the butt who chases hunters off his wildlife preserve."

"Oh, McAdam," grunted the officer coldly. "What are

you doing back here after everything's all closed up?"

"Just resting off a migraine headache. I was carrying some supplies out of the feed store when it came over me, and I didn't want to start driving until the lights stopped dancing in front of my eyes. But now I'm all right and ready to leave, so—"

"Wait a minute. Did you see a kid back here?"

"What did he do?"

"He's a runaway. Have you seen him?"

"Well, what did he look like?"

"Scrawny. About twelve years old. He had a blue baseball cap on, a red T-shirt, jeans, and sneakers."

"What's he running from?"

The officer's voice turned gruff. "You are a very difficult man, you know that?"

"I'm only asking."

"Stay there, McAdam."

Jeremy heard the deputy get out of his patrol car and his footsteps scuffing along the ground. He saw the play of a flashlight coming through the tarp above him. Then the light went away. The officer moved farther off, and the lid of the Dumpster creaked as it went up on its hinges again.

"He could have been hiding in this till everything closed down, then come out while you were parked here." Now the footsteps were coming back. The officer was practically standing over him. "So maybe he even crawled in under this tarp while you were . . . resting your eyes. Let's have a look."

"Hold it!" the deep voice boomed.

The boy heard the pickup's door open . Then a large hand pressed down on him through the tarp.

"You need my permission to look through my property."

"Not when it's on the open back of a truck."

"If it was open you wouldn't have to pick up the tarp."

"You got a problem with my seeing what's under there, McAdam?"

"That depends. Why don't you tell me about this boy?"

There was a long pause before the officer drew a loud breath. He sounded less angry now, almost as if he needed someone to confide in. "About an hour ago we arrested a woman in the market for shoplifting. She said her son was outside with her boyfriend, who was gassing up the car. The boyfriend said the kid ran off when he saw that his mother was about to be arrested. We told the guy to search for him and then come out to the station. The boyfriend showed up later and didn't seem at all unhappy that he couldn't find the kid. On a hunch we checked the boyfriend out and he'd just gotten out of jail a few weeks ago. Guess what he'd been in for?"

"Beating up the boy?"

"No, the mother. They had to wire her jaw and reconstruct part of her face. But it was the kid who called the police and testified against him at the trial."

"So the youngster's running for his life?"

The officer sighed. "The boyfriend swears up and down that he doesn't blame the kid for having stuck up for his mom. He says he's reformed; he's off the drugs and booze. The mother says she believes him."

"Do you trust the judgment of a woman who just shoplifted in front of her own son?"

"No, and if you ask me the guy made her do it. Some kind of a crazy dare. But then she paid for the packs of cigarettes and the store dropped the charges as long as she's on her way out of the area."

"So that's all that counts? That the problem goes somewhere else?"

The deputy let out another sigh. "They've got a battered woman's shelter down in Medford," he said. "The social worker at the place told me it happens like this a lot. A woman moves to a different town and nobody's supposed to know where she's living, but somehow the man does find out. He comes to her with a song and a dance, and off she goes with him! Then a few days or a few weeks later it's the same old merry-go-round, only maybe worse. And there's nothing that anyone can do about it. Now, do I get to look under this tarp or not?"

"If you can show me a search warrant, sure."

"Standing on your rights?" snorted the officer.

"That's what rights are there for."

"For a moment there I forgot who I was dealing with—the man who'd rather sue his neighbors than get

13

along with them. Use your head, McAdam. That kid is only twelve years old, for God's sake. How is he going to take care of himself?"

"I don't know. But if he gets his own jaw smashed in by his mother's boyfriend, how is that an improvement over being on his own?"

"I don't say it is. But that's not up to us, is it?"

Jeremy heard a long silence. Then "No . . . I guess not." And the protective hand came off the tarp. He was caught. Trapped!

Then the man said, "All right, I did see him. He was down that way, by the gun store, scooting up the fence."

"Proud of yourself for stalling me, McAdam?"

"Are you sure you're not glad I did?"

"Go on," growled the officer. "Take off."

CHAPTER

Tightly huddled between the bags of animal feed, Jeremy didn't know whether to be grateful to the driver or not. This man who was driving him away from the cop sounded weird, like he had a "history" of his own.

He'd heard plenty of warnings about so-called "good guys" during the weeks when he was living in Juvenile Hall down in the city. That was where some social worker had dumped him while his mother was in the hospital recovering from her beating and there was no one to take him in. What a place!

Mostly Juvie Hall, as they called it, was like a jail for kids who'd gotten into too much trouble with the law or the school or with foster parents. And just like prisoners in a real lockup, the kids told each other stories about what it was like to be on the outside— especially when they were on their own. A runaway kid would be living on the streets or hanging out at the bus terminal. And suddenly there'd be a "good guy" popping up out of nowhere, offering to help out with a meal and a place to stay. But if you took the guy up on it, look out! You were in for some heavy things that you weren't *ever* counting on.

No, he'd be real careful about this McAdam. Better still, he'd get off this truck as soon as it stopped for a light somewhere.

But that wasn't happening. The truck was going on and on. Weren't there any traffic lights around here? And where were they headed? Forget about hiding, Jeremy told himself. I better see what's going on.

He lifted the tarp . . . and groaned. Except for some oncoming headlights, the road was black.

There was *nothing* there. No stores, no streets. And the cars going the other way were zooming by at about seventy miles an hour. Even if he got off this thing and stuck his thumb out, who would stop?

What a dummy I was, losing it back there at the supermarket! Jeremy thought. It was seeing that cop bringing Mom out of that store with *handcuffs* on, like she was a *crook!* That, and watching Ed at the gas pump, just standing there smoking his cigarette and acting so surprised and innocent! Well, Ed was the thief, not her! Ed could get her to do anything!

Still, it was stupid of him to run off like that. All he had to do was stay with Ed till the cops let Mom go and they all drove down to the Bronx. *Then* he could have taken off. That way it would just be a subway ride down to East Harlem to find that kid Martinez and get him to lend Jeremy his gun.

Well, that was still going to happen! Jeremy wasn't giving Ed any more chances to beat his mother's face in. One way or another, Jeremy promised himself, I'm getting down there tonight and putting an end to this once and for all.

The truck was slowing down at last, starting a right turn onto a much narrower road. Here was Jeremy's chance to go over the tailgate without hurting himself when he landed.

Jeremy started to rise from his crouch and darted a quick look to either side. On his left was a tiny building set back from the corner. Above its dimly lit window a sign said DEVIL'S GORGE GENERAL STORE. And a shopper on her way to her car was about to see him.

It was too late now to make a decision whether to jump or not. The turning truck was already picking up speed. Jeremy sank back. For the next few hundred feet the ground was fairly level. Then the truck shifted into a lower gear and began to climb.

Up and up it went, passing a scattering of small houses. He saw television screens flickering in some windows, fireplaces in others. Yet it was the dark shape of a tiny tricycle up on a porch that for some reason made him feel lonely.

With each twist and turn the distances between the houses grew. At last there was nothing but forest closing in on a road that was not much wider than the truck itself.

And still they climbed.

Jeremy began to notice the sound the tires were making on the bumpy road. Hey, no more pavement, he realized. That's dirt down there! If I fall when I hit the ground it's no big deal. There's hardly any drop at all if I let the tailgate down first and crawl out on it.

Jeremy was in the middle of doing that when the truck hit a deep pothole. The jolt sent him skidding sideways off the bed of the truck and across the flattened tailgate. Half his body shot out over the side of the road.

But there wasn't any side of the road. There was only a cliff! And the vast, dark mouth of the Devil's Gorge waited for his fall.

Jeremy's wildly flailing hand grabbed a small chain connecting the side of the truck to a ring on the tailgate. But that alone wasn't enough to break the force of Jeremy's slide. He was losing hold and going off feet first!

Desperately reaching over his head with the other hand, Jeremy seized the chain and tugged. Now the first hand grabbed again. Little by little, Jeremy's straining arms pulled him close enough to get first one leg, then the other, back onto the truck bed.

He was still working his way into the pickup when the ground leveled off. Panting and in a cold sweat, Jeremy flipped the tailgate up and scurried under the tarp.

The truck rattled over a wooden bridge that crossed a dried-out creek. Then it moved into a small clearing in the woods and drew up alongside a feed barn that was no larger than a storage shed. The motor was shut off.

But by that time, Jeremy was no longer aboard. Dropping quickly to the ground even before the truck had stopped, he ducked low and made for the woods a few feet away. He was already in hiding when McAdam got out of the pickup.

"Sorry I didn't stop earlier to let you come sit up front with me," said the man as he went around to the back. "At first I thought it better not to risk having anyone see you. But then I . . . well, I had some things to think about. Anyway, come on out from there, son. Let's go have a couple of cups of cocoa and talk things over."

Yeah, sure, thought Jeremy, crouched down in the bushes. Cocoa and some talk. Only what *else* did the old guy have in mind?

Careful not to make any noise, he watched the man stare at the tarp, then reach out and lift it. The old guy rubbed his beard as if in puzzlement. Then he started to glance around. He was turning this way!

A stab of fear sent Jeremy's fingers searching over the ground. His right hand closed around a rock the size of a big fist. Jeremy crouched behind a tree, ready to lunge.

But none of this was necessary. Jeremy heard a grunt,

then heavy steps moving away, and a door creaking open. He took a chance and peeked. McAdam, with one of the huge feed bags slung over his shoulder, was trudging into the little barn. A moment later he came out, holding his back and looking tired. But all the same, he went right back to the pickup and hefted another bag.

Jeremy thought it was pretty cool for an old guy to be going at it like that. You sure wouldn't catch Mom's boyfriend lifting just one of those sacks without telling the world how it was going to give him a hernia unless everybody immediately rushed over to do it for him.

Jeremy began to wonder if this man wasn't okay after all. Maybe the only thing McAdam *did* want was to make sure he was all right. From the way he'd talked to that deputy it seemed like the cops weren't his favorite people. And the man had stuck up for him when he'd heard what Ed had done to Mom's jaw.

Yeah, but why did both of them make it sound like Mom was *stupid?* They didn't know all the good things about her, so where did they come off talking like that? The hell with both of them, then. Jeremy wasn't going to feel one bit sorry about taking this guy's truck.

Not that this was really going to be *stealing,* Jeremy told himself. It wasn't like he was going to *sell* it, just take it to where he had a good chance of getting a ride to the city. To some truckers' diner maybe, like the one outside Medford where his mom had been waitressing. Or maybe, if he really got the hang of driving this rig, he'd take it out on the highway and go all the way down! Then he'd just leave it safe someplace and call the cops to tell them where to find it.

At last the door to the barn clicked shut. McAdam walked toward a dark cabin about fifty feet away. Stepping away from the tree, the boy watched him go inside.

Now!

It was a quick dash to the passenger's door—the side of the truck that wasn't facing the house. No light went on overhead when he opened it, and his hand soon found the ignition key.

Good. Climbing onto the seat, he crawled past the stick shift and dropped his legs beneath the wheel. But when his feet swung out, they couldn't reach the pedals.

Calm down, Jeremy told himself. Not every driver is built like a basketball pro. There's got to be some way to move the seat into shrimp position. He tugged at a latch on the underside of the seat, heard a click, and slid right up to the front.

Jeremy wasn't worried about handling the wheel, not after all those times when he'd steered the car from the passenger's side because Ed was too drunk to keep it from swaying all over the road. And he knew from watching the driver of his school bus what the stick was for and why there were three pedals down on the floor. But which pedal worked the clutch? And what were the moves you made with your hand to go through all those gears?

You'll figure it out, Jeremy told himself. Just calm

down and take it from here. First thing is, you get the engine going. Turn the key.

The starter made such a loud grinding noise·that Jeremy shut it off quickly and darted a look at the cabin.

There was a light now in one of the windows, but McAdam had his back to it. The boy heard some music go on—dead-guy stuff that must have been written hundreds of years ago. Lots of instruments playing loud. Good.

Maybe I have to turn the starter on and give it gas at the same time, he thought. But when he tried that, the pickup lurched ahead like a bucking rodeo horse. His chest went into the steering wheel, his foot fell off the pedal, and the engine conked out. Jeremy realized there was no way he could steer this truck down a road where there was a wall of rock on one side and a whole lot of nothing at all on the other.

Okay, so driving was out. He'd just have to walk, that's all. Never mind that it was getting windy out, not to mention that he was hungry. Back in that garbage bin among the rotting food, he'd lost his appetite. But now that he noticed it, he was so starved that his stomach hurt.

Stop thinking about that, he ordered himself. What he really needed was something he could see by. Jeremy ran his hand along the dashboard until he found the glove compartment, then opened it and felt inside. No flashlight or cigarette lighter, or even a book of matches. There was just a long thin object in a wrapper. And when the boy's thumb pressed down on it, he knew in an instant that it couldn't be anything else but a Tootsie Roll—a big one!

Now this was more like it! Jeremy tore off the wrapper as he got out of the truck. One end of it was already in his mouth when the darkness just ahead of him was filled with an oncoming mass of furry blackness.

Petrified, Jeremy fell back against the open door. As it slammed behind his back, two gigantic paws reared up to plant themselves on either side of him. Round eyes, no larger than marbles, stared into his. There was a strong whiff of animal breath as the great mouth opened. Then—*plunk!*—the bear ate the Tootsie Roll.

Jeremy's legs grew weak. He couldn't run now even if he had the chance to. That big mouth was opening again. What was it going to eat next?

Me?

But the great beast only licked its muzzle. Then, dropping to all fours again, it turned away. Jeremy watched it lumber over to the cabin, then rise to scratch at the kitchen window.

McAdam opened it, saying, "Oh Mitzi! I'm so sorry. I forgot to give you your treat. Be right out."

This is weird, thought Jeremy. Big-time *weird!*

Both man and bear were coming toward him now. If Jeremy had to hide again, it was going to be with a door between him and that bear! Pulling himself together, he sprang for the barn.

It was an old building made of logs, and there were several small chinks in the wall. Jeremy put an eye to one of them and watched McAdam go into the truck for the Tootsie Roll.

The old guy came out empty-handed, but chuckling. "Why, you clever bear, you. All by yourself you actually opened the door, then went into the glove compartment and took out your treat. Of course, I always did know you were intelligent. But what really impresses me is how you've suddenly developed such good manners. You closed everything up when you were through!" He stroked the furry head. "So, Mitzi, I'll tell you what. Since you're being such a . . . well, such a *person* . . . I'm going to let you come into the house just this one last time. But don't you dare start your old tricks again, pulling the cereal boxes off my shelves or climbing onto the only two chairs you haven't broken. Because if you don't behave, then out you go."

And off they lumbered together into the house.

Jeremy slipped out of the barn. There were no stars overhead, nothing to see by. And the trees were a darker mass all around him. He'd just have to be careful not to wander into them as he tried to find the road.

Making one careful step after another, Jeremy felt his way along in the darkness. Little by little he grew more sure of himself, and he began taking bigger steps. He even started to plan how he was going to finish off Ed. It had to be in a way that no one, especially his mother, would suspect him.

"I'll give her some time to get over it and see how much better off she is without him," Jeremy said out loud. "Then we'll come back to Medford so she can go back to work in the diner and start taking some classes at that school again. But if the job gets to be too much for her while she's learning to become a nurse, that's no sweat either. 'Cause meanwhile I'll be getting bigger all the time and I'll take care of—"

Jeremy was so busy talking and planning, he hadn't noticed the ground beginning to tilt slightly. Now he raised his left foot, and it came down on . . . *nothing!* Jeremy's frantically waving arms couldn't give him back his balance. There wasn't anything to grab hold of. He toppled sideways, with a vision of the gorge bursting in his mind. The shriek that flew from his mouth was the fear of death put into sound. Death could not be put aside till old age. Death was coming *now.*

CHAPTER

But almost as soon as the fall started, Jeremy struck ground again, landing on his side. Amazement kept him from doing anything to stop his slide over roots and rocks. The short tumble ended when he rolled onto a damp bed of pebbles. He lay there for a few moments, breathing heavily and feeling lucky. A few bangs and scrapes were nothing compared to what he had just imagined.

As the sound of his own panting died away, Jeremy heard a rapid fluttering and a low rumble. Looking up, he saw that he was lying near the bottom of the wooden bridge the pickup had crossed earlier. The sounds were coming from just underneath its timbers and growing more agitated. Then all at once black creatures were rocketing past him, so closely that their breeze parted his hair. Jeremy recognized them from vampire movies and a chill shot up his spine.

Bats! Those were *bats!*

A wing tip brushed his face and Jeremy pulled back in disgust, trying to wipe away the sticky feeling where he'd been touched. He had to get away from here!

Jeremy scrambled up the embankment on his hands and knees. By the time he reached the top, he had made up his mind that tonight he wasn't going anywhere. He headed back toward the feed barn.

The light from the kitchen window didn't spill very far into the darkness beyond the cabin. But now something much more powerful was reaching out to Jeremy: the smell of hot cocoa. He sniffed it as he ducked past the far side of the truck. And looking over the hood he saw the steaming mug that rested on the windowsill.

"Now, Mitzi," he heard McAdam say, "stay away from that cherry-blueberry pie. It isn't for you. I gave you some when I baked it this morning."

The boy caught on in a hurry. It was obvious McAdam knew he was out here. Was this a trap?

A plate loaded to the edges with pie was set down on the sill beside the cocoa, a big creamy glob of ice cream on top. McAdam turned away from the window.

Jeremy began to plan. He would have to sneak up to the cabin, then inch himself along the wall to the window. Fading back into the trees, he made a wide circle around the nearest corner of the building. There was a window on this side too, a tinier one that probably belonged to the bathroom. But it was dark. He went up to the wall boldly, plastered himself against the log frame, and began to move. Closer. Closer. The smell of that cocoa was almost like tasting it. And that humongous slice of pie a la mode was drawing him along like a magnet!

Jeremy made it to the near edge of the window. He was almost beside the food. All he had to do now—if McAdam didn't make a grab for his arm—was just reach out.

He heard a grunt, low and animal-like, and it sent a stab of fear shooting into his chest. Jeremy's breathing stopped. Even his stomach grew quiet. And, in spite of the sharp wind, he began to sweat.

Calm down, Jeremy told himself sternly. That bear is just like this guy's big pet dog, right?

But what if it was only tame for *him?* Jeremy had seen dogs that would take off your hand if you came too close. And where *was* the old guy, anyway? Right up against the other side of this wall, waiting for Jeremy to make his move? I'd better look before I grab, he decided.

The first thing he saw was McAdam in the next room kneeling before a stone fireplace. The man had a long metal rod in his hand and was poking at logs that were starting to burn.

Great, but that still left the bear. He moved his head a little further. *She* was at the kitchen table, with her behind on the floor, holding a baking pan in her paws while she licked it clean. Jeremy figured he was safe.

The first body-warming gulp of cocoa was splashing down his throat when the old man sang out, "In a minute or two, son, this fire's going to make the house as warm as toast. Good thing, too. The night air can get real wintry this time of the year up here on the mountain. Nicer to breathe, though, than in the valley. No gas fumes in it. Listen, if that cocoa has cooled off too much, I can heat up some more."

Jeremy made a grab for the pie just as McAdam, still holding that poker, turned to look at him. Perhaps the old man noticed the wary look in his visitor's eyes. Setting the rod down as he rose, he went only as far as the doorway to the kitchen.

"I don't have any idea what's making you leery of me," the man said softly. "But I learned long ago that there's always an important reason why people feel the way they do. So I leave it to you to show me what I can do to help you feel easier. And meanwhile, if you're still hungry when you finish all that—"

The clatter of the baking pan landing on the floor interrupted him. With a swipe of her paw, Mitzi had sent it skidding off the table.

"Bad girl!" McAdam cried. But the bear paid no attention. She already had her eye on a half-finished package of bread on top of the refrigerator. Rising to her full height, she popped the loaf into her mouth, wrapper and all.

Suddenly, Jeremy realized how much food he had been cramming into his own mouth. McAdam, turning from the bear to the boy, must have noticed the same thing. He took a step back in order to see them both at the same time, then leaned back on his heels and roared with laughter.

The bear didn't seem a bit offended. But the boy suddenly couldn't get rid of what was still in his mouth fast enough. All of that cherry-blueberry pie was poison to him now! Spitting it all out on the ground, he slapped the plate back down on the sill and glared at the man. People could not make fun of him. Not kids, not grown-ups—and especially not strangers pretending to be good guys!

McAdam seemed to realize that he'd made a big mistake. His laughter was cut short and his smile vanished. "That was unkind, and I'm sorry," he said. "It just looked to me as if you and Mitzi share the same wonderful appetite. Actually, I envy it. You'd be surprised at how little a big man like me eats nowadays. Am I forgiven?"

Jeremy gave him a smoldering look, then warned himself to calm down. "Yeah," he half growled.

McAdam seemed happy to settle for that and brightened at once. "Well, anyway, hello. We can't shake hands from this distance, but maybe we can introduce ourselves. I think you've already heard the last part of my name, McAdam. My first name is Aaron."

Jeremy nodded slowly, but that was all. What does he want from me, he asked himself.

The man was obviously waiting for something. Finally, he said, "Want to tell me yours?"

The boy thought it over. Was there anything to lose

here? If so, he couldn't see it. Just in case, though, he wasn't going to give away too much. "Jeremy."

"Jeremy what?"

The boy looked away. "Got a lot of last names. You pick one."

A cold blast of November wind suddenly caught him between the shoulders. He tried not to let the old guy see him shiver.

"No, Jeremy's fine," McAdam replied. "And I'll tell you what. You decide where to stay tonight. It could be in the barn, in the pickup . . . or here on the couch by the fireplace. Either way I'll give you a warm blanket. But if you come inside, we might be able to find out if there's some way I can help you with that problem of yours."

Jeremy considered McAdam's offer. It could be a lie, of course, but maybe he ought to check it out. Except for laughing at him, so far the old guy hadn't made a false move. And even the laughter was honest, at least—the man wasn't playing at being the nice guy. Maybe he even meant it when he apologized. Still . . .

"I'm not going in no house with no bear," he said.

"Well, that settles it then!" said McAdam. "Come on, Mitzi! Now that you're going to be a mother it's high time to remember you belong in a den of your own. Out you go."

He led the way to the cabin door but the bear merely looked at him from the kitchen and wouldn't budge.

"What's this? Are you being naughty again?" He clapped his hands together loudly.

This got a little action. The bear very slowly padded halfway out of the kitchen. But there she stopped.

McAdam grew firm. "Mitzi, did you hear me? We've found you a perfectly nice ledge to go under. And you'd better start getting it prepared for your cubs."

Jeremy watched the reluctant bear's rear end pass ever so slowly out of the kitchen. Then a new thought struck him—hard. That animal was about to show up where *he* was.

"Wait a second! Keep her there till I tell you!" he cried, starting to boost himself onto the sill. He got one leg over it. "Okay."

Now Jeremy could see through the whole length of the little cabin. Mitzi was at the open door and she seemed to realize that the odds against her staying were hopeless. She leaned against McAdam on her way through. Was that to punish him with a little push or because she wanted him to stroke her? Jeremy couldn't tell, but McAdam passed a gentle hand over her coat before he closed the door. "All clear, son."

Jeremy had never believed in waiting around for important things to happen, especially when he was in a major hurry. Passing through the kitchen, he went straight up to McAdam and said, "Listen, I really need to get down to the city as soon as I can."

McAdam seemed puzzled. "What city? Oh, you mean New York? That's a long way from here."

33

"I know that," Jeremy replied evenly. "But you said you wanted to help, right?"

"What I said was we'd talk about it. Do you have family there?"

This conversation was beginning to feel like a mistake. But Jeremy had started it and now he needed to give *some* answer. He nodded, hoping the questions would stop.

But the man kept at it. "Who?"

"The cop told you who."

A bewildered expression crossed McAdam's face. "You want to go back to your *mother?* Do you think it's safe?"

This was getting harder and harder. Certainly Jeremy couldn't tell the man what he was planning to do in the city to make everything "safe." So he just dug his hands into his pockets and shrugged.

But McAdam was marching to a wall full of bookshelves, saying, "Let me call the police then. Your mother still might be at the station house."

"Hold on a minute!" Jeremy cried in protest. "I didn't say I want to call her right now. Not with *him* still around!"

McAdam took his hand off the receiver. "Do you really think he's going to leave?"

"Yeah. Oh, yeah."

"When do you expect that might be?"

"Soon." *Count on it,* Jeremy promised himself.

McAdam seemed to grow thoughtful and tired at

the same time. Jeremy watched him trudge over to a leather armchair and toss his long body into it.

"How long were they together?" he asked after awhile.

Jeremy had to think back. What grade was he in when she came home one night with his *new father?* "Four years," he said.

McAdam had been unlacing his thick boots. Pulling them off seemed to relax him. "Did this fellow always beat her?"

"He wasn't too bad in the beginning—just a few arguments now and then," Jeremy said slowly. "But then he accused her of some real bad stuff."

McAdam looked up. "But that was all lies!" Jeremy insisted quickly. "Ed was just pulling all that to cover up the stuff that *he'd* done. He'd make up stories, and then he'd start believing they were true. Then he'd blow the roof off."

"What about your mother? Did he talk her into believing them, too?"

"What are you talking about?" Jeremy demanded sharply. "Are you asking me if my mother's being brainwashed, like you see in those war movies? No way! Sometimes she'll apologize for something, to keep him quiet. But that's it." Growing silent for a moment, he added, "Mostly she just doesn't argue with him. She waits till things calm down."

"But in between he hits her?"

"Yeah." Jeremy could see where this was going, and he stared at the floor. "Sometimes."

Sure enough, the old guy followed up with, "Then what makes you think this is going to end anytime soon?"

"Because I *know.*"

McAdam was careful. "Well, in the meantime, is there a place in the city where you can stay?"

"I'll get by." Jeremy began to fidget. "Look, is it okay if we don't talk anymore?" His agitated gaze traveled around the room and took in the steps of a ladder leading up to a little sleeping loft near the roof of the cabin. "Got a TV up there?"

"Afraid not."

"I'll stay here then, " Jeremy said, spotting a small set in a corner.

"That one doesn't work. Why don't you pull that rocking chair up over here by the fire and let me show you the oldest television set in the world." He jostled a log with the poker and sent a storm of sparks flying up to the chimney.

Halfheartedly, Jeremy joined him. McAdam shut off the little lamp between them and they both stared into the blaze.

"I'm convinced that here is where all the world's storytelling began," McAdam told Jeremy. "At the day's end our ancestors gathered around the campfires for closeness as well as warmth. They had their backs to the night, and looking into the blaze they began to grow thoughtful. Then someone spoke up. He . . . or she . . . didn't know many words perhaps. But he wanted to share something that had happened.

Perhaps it was about something he'd learned, something that might help them all to survive and deserved to be remembered. As the others listened they saw images in the flames of what he was describing. I think those visions were like flames themselves. They burned into the imaginations of the audience. Then everybody fed those remembrances, just like they all fed the fire. And out of this grew the stories that would help make remembering easier."

"Did you read this somewhere or are you guessing?" Jeremy asked carefully.

McAdam laughed. "No, just guessing. And even if I'd read it, that would only be someone else's guess."

"Well, since that's what we're doing," put in the boy after awhile, "I don't think it was a bunch of memories that started the stories off."

"What then?"

"I think it was mysteries. Like trying to puzzle things out." Jeremy fell silent for a moment. "And also finding ways to think about scary things so they wouldn't be bothered about them all the time."

McAdam grew thoughtful. Then he sighed. "You know, son, you're probably right."

"Listen, I've got to tell you something," Jeremy muttered.

"What's that?"

"Two things," he said with growing heat. "First off, my mother is no dumbbell, no matter what you and that cop think about her."

McAdam leaned forward quickly. "I'm sorry if in any way I—"

"And the next is I'm not anybody's *son* but hers! So don't call me that."

"I understand."

"Okay." With that settled, Jeremy relaxed. "Listen, thanks for everything. I mean that."

"You're welcome."

"Only right now I'm beat, you know what I'm saying?" To prove his point Jeremy added a loud yawn.

"Sounds like my exit cue," said McAdam, pushing himself out of the easy chair and heading for the ladder. "The sofa's comfortable, and you can just take the blanket down off the back of it. Think that will be enough?"

With a drowsy grunt, the boy got up and crossed the room. Without so much as kicking his shoes off, he stretched out on his back, pulling the blanket down over him. "I'm fine."

"All right, then." McAdam had already started climbing. He paused on the second step. "Since I didn't say this before, I want you to know that I admire your spirit." Now he grinned. "Also the speed you used going up that fence at the shopping center."

"Yeah, but I didn't make it over."

"Who knows, maybe it worked out for the best this way. Well, good night, youngster. Tomorrow we'll take another look at everything." He returned to his climbing.

"'Night," Jeremy replied groggily, as if he was dropping off. But he was only waiting for the old guy to settle in and fall asleep.

It seemed to take forever before all the creaking and moving around overhead came to a stop. Even then he had to give it a little more time before getting up again. For all he knew the guy could just be lying there with his eyes wide open, too.

Only how could he keep from being bored to death, meanwhile? Staring at the burning logs, Jeremy made up a story about a kid with the power to make the greatest speeches in the world. First the kid won a national debating contest and got to meet the president in Washington. Then he convinced the government to turn over all the abandoned houses to homeless people. But the places were in terrible shape and so were a lot of the people. So then he had to talk them into taking a chance on believing in themselves and helping each other get everything fixed. But then all the neighborhood drug dealers got mad. They needed to have those abandoned houses stay like they were, or else their druggie customers would lose the hiding places where they went to shoot up. So now he had to convince the dealers to lay off. But considering how crazy for money *those* guys were, that was going to be the toughest job of all.

It was so tough, in fact, that this part of the story began to repeat itself over and over. Without knowing it, he was drifting off . . .

A sudden snort jarred him awake—and at last Jeremy heard McAdam's heavy, even breathing. Bounding to his feet and taking the blanket with him, Jeremy rushed to the phone.

It rang a few times before Martinez answered. "How you doing?" Jeremy whispered.

"Who is this? Speak up, I can't hear you."

"It's Jeremy Utrillo."

"Hey, your voice is funny. Where you callin' from?"

"I'm still upstate, but I'm coming down tomorrow, and I need a big favor. Can I stay with you?"

There was a silence. "Yeah, okay. But I gotta tell you that it sucks down here. And I'm disappointed in you, Utrillo. You told me that as soon as your mom got a place of her own, you were gonna have *me* come out there!"

"Yeah, well it didn't work out. That creep Ed showed up at the shelter and she went with him. She went back with the guy, can you believe that? But I'm gonna waste him. You know, like we talked about when we were in Juvie Hall together."

There was another silence. "Hey, come on, we were just, you know, making up stuff to pass the time," Martinez said at last.

"But you told me you've *killed* guys."

"Yeah. Well, I shot back at guys, that's for sure. But I didn't *look* to do it. That was stuff I *had* to do to save my life."

"Are you gonna lend me a gun or not?"

"Hey, you want to know the reason why you got me

just now? There's guys after me! I don't even keep the lights on anymore. Fact is, I thought you was one of them calling to tell me, 'You not coming out, Martinez? That's okay. One of these nights we'll be coming in after *you.*' Jeremy, listen, you can come here if you want to. But that's crazy now. The only thing that's keeping me alive down here in this basement is that when my brother was the super here he put metal gates over the windows and all kinds of locks on the door. But where's my brother now? He's *dead!* Listen, I'm your friend and I'm telling you to find some way to stay up there. Believe me, you don't want any part of this."

Martinez paused. Then he said, "So what are you gonna do?"

"I don't know."

"Good luck."

"Yeah . . . you too."

As he was hanging up, Jeremy thought he heard a sigh. He darted a suspicious glance at the sleeping loft. But there was nothing to see, nothing to hear. Perhaps he'd let that sigh out himself. There was, after all, a real heavy feeling pressing down on his chest.

CHAPTER

4

The sizzle of eggs and smell of frying bacon entered Jeremy's dream of being back in the diner where his mother used to work. But the meal never came and he grew hungrier and hungrier.

"Up and at 'em!" a voice sang out cheerily. "Nobody's going to feed you lying on your back."

That woke him. But starved or not, Jeremy was still woozy-headed as he very slowly lowered his sneaker-covered feet to the floor.

McAdam looked in from the kitchen. "Morning, youngster. I see you're dressed already."

Ignoring McAdam's teasing, Jeremy shuffled blearily past him on his way to a little door. McAdam was saying something about using the kitchen sink for washing up instead of the bathroom, but Jeremy paid no attention. A little bleating sound came from behind the door as he started to pull it open.

"There's a *deer* in there!" he exclaimed, backing

away quickly.

"That's what I was trying to tell you," said McAdam, setting plates and silverware on the table. "And you mustn't scare him. He's very young and shy. Anyway, I'm sure you're glad that he's not another bear." McAdam couldn't resist a little grin as he shoveled out bacon and eggs. When Jeremy glared at him, he said. "The food is on the table. Come and dig in."

Jeremy looked at his filled plate as he sat down, but he didn't pick up the fork. He felt as if his face was on fire. "I wasn't scared," he insisted. "Just surprised, that's all. But why I should be surprised in *this* place, I really don't know."

"That's the spirit!" McAdam said, sliding into the chair across from him and starting to eat. "Now I wonder if you noticed anything unusual about that fawn?"

Jeremy looked up from poking at the eggs. "Aside from being in your bathroom?"

"Right."

"Well, I didn't see him munching any Tootsie Rolls. Could that be it?"

"No, smart guy. You saw how little he is. I meant his age. Mostly they're born in the spring and they've been weaned by now. It's very rare to find one that's so young this late in the year. But he was half-starved when I found him, so he could be a little older than he looks. Not by much though. He still has those beautiful spots. Did you notice?"

"It wasn't entirely on my mind," said the boy.

44

McAdam sat back, looking amused. "You've probably decided by now that I'm a bit off my rocker."

"Who, me?"

"Yes, *you*. But that's all right. Most people around here think I am."

Jeremy stopped eating. "And you don't care?"

"Sometimes. But then I remind myself that there's always a reason for what I do. It got really cold last night, as you know, and I was worried what that might do to that run-down baby's resistance. My reason for putting him in the bathroom is because the tile is easy to clean. Still, I don't want to keep him in a space that small. So in a little while he'll go back into the pen where I took him from."

McAdam fell silent, then glanced up from his food. "Would you like to help me?"

"How?" Setting down his glass of milk, Jeremy shot him a look. "By cleaning up after that deer?"

McAdam chuckled. "Oh, I wouldn't inflict that on you. But there are other things to do that aren't nearly as messy. And you might even discover that this wildlife refuge is an interesting place if you stick around a little while."

"Yeah, well, I don't think that's such a hot idea. If some cop finds me here that'll be trouble for you." Jeremy got up.

McAdam got to his feet and looked Jeremy in the eye. "I appreciate the concern but that would be *my* problem."

"And I appreciate your worrying about me, I really do. But I gotta go now." Pausing a moment, he stuck out his hand and McAdam took it.

"Look," Jeremy went on, "I don't want to say that you've been a good guy, because where I've been that means something a whole lot different than . . . Well, anyway thanks for everything. If they catch me I'm not going to tell them you helped me or that I was here or anything. Good luck with all the deer and the bears and whatever." He turned to go.

"Good luck to you, too. I just wish I knew how you intend to take care of yourself."

"Don't let it bother you. I'll manage." Jeremy strutted through the cabin to the door. "Believe me, I've been around."

"I *do* believe you," McAdam said, a worried frown creasing his face as he followed the boy outside. "But just let me ask you one question. How are you fixed for money?"

Jeremy stopped short. "Why?"

"Help me with some chores this morning and I'll pay you . . . let's see . . . twenty dollars sounds about right. What do you think?"

Twenty bucks? While hiding in that garbage bin yesterday, Jeremy had gone through his pocket money over and over. The final haul was a dollar and forty-two cents. That wouldn't even buy him a hamburger. He turned around, wondering if there was a catch here. "How long's it gonna take me? Just this morning, right?"

"Right. Then I'll put you back under the tarp and drive you to the bus."

"How much is a ticket to the city?"

"Twenty should cover it. You might even have a couple of dollars left over."

"Is some policeman gonna be looking for me at the bus station?"

"I don't know. Probably not." McAdam waited a beat and added, "It isn't as if they're hunting a murderer."

Murderer. The word stung Jeremy like a maddened bee. It scared him—and it made him suspicious too. What did McAdam know? Had he only been pretending to be asleep while Jeremy talked on the phone last night? Then the man would know all his plans! McAdam could have him arrested, or at least stopped. Maybe he'd call the cops and have them warn Ed!

But behind that white beard the old guy wasn't showing anything. His eyes were steady and mild, as if he didn't have the slightest idea he'd said anything at all to shake the boy up.

Jeremy pulled himself together. If this guy could fake looking innocent, so could he. Meanwhile, there was this offer of twenty bucks. That was no fortune, but at least it would buy a bus ticket. It could even get him something better than that! He could find some other way to make it down to the city and use the cash to buy a warm jacket from one of those secondhand army stores and maybe a couple of meals at McDonald's, too. Then he'd look around for some boarded up building where he could crash for a few nights while he figured out what to do about a gun.

"Okay," he said at last.

"Good," declared McAdam. "Now before we get

started, duck back into the cabin and bring me one of the small sofa cushions."

Jeremy did as he was told without asking questions. "Let's go," said McAdam, and they headed off toward an outcropping of trees and rock.

Following a footpath through the woods, they soon came out into a large open field that held an animal pen. The pen was surrounded by a mesh fence and divided in two parts, one much larger than the other. Inside the bigger section, a fully grown deer with six points on his antlers hobbled about on a splint.

"I want to check out the buck's fracture," McAdam said, stuffing the pillow under his woolen shirt. "Last time I tried touching that leg, though, I got a kick in the ribs that I felt for days. It was my fault, I wasn't careful enough. Deer are like horses in some ways, you know."

"So what do you want me to do?" Jeremy asked.

"Nothing till I'm in the pen and he starts getting used to my being there. Then—you see that pile of branches and leaves over there?" McAdam pointed to a mound of brush at the edge of the woods.

"Uh-huh."

"I collected them from white cedar trees, a deer's favorite kind. They love the smell. Something like the way you are with hot cocoa."

McAdam had cracked a friendly smile, but Jeremy refused to take the bait. "So you want me to bring that stuff here?" he asked.

"Yup. Drag about half of the pile up against the fence.

Then walk away from the buck so that he stops being concerned about you. All right?"

"If you say so, boss."

"You like getting the last word in, don't you?"

"*Yup*," replied Jeremy, imitating him. As he walked off, grinning thinly, he heard the gate to the pen opening and closing, but no footsteps. When he got to the brush pile, he looked back. McAdam was standing motionless by the gate. From the distance of half a basketball court away the deer eyed him carefully. Finally it shifted its attention to Jeremy himself, who was bending over the pile, gathering and dragging.

A fallen branch cracked underfoot. The loud sound startled the animal. Its head snapped and it bolted into a limping run for the safety of a small lean-to inside the enclosure. It went in backward, nostrils wide and antlers lowered.

The flat of McAdam's hand went down and up slowly—a signal to work more carefully. If his arms hadn't been full, Jeremy would have sent a signal of his own, with his palms up in the air. *I'm doing the best I can, you know. You wanted this stuff? Here it is.*

Inside the pen, both man and deer seemed to get the idea. They remained fixed in place while he walked back and forth, heaping brush against the fence. Finished at last, Jeremy marched off into the trees, then turned and grew still. The deer relaxed. Hobbling to the fence, it blissfully poked its nose through the wire and into the fragrant brush.

Jeremy watched McAdam cross slowly to the animal,

kneel beside it, and grow still again. When he finally reached for the injured leg, it was with a smooth roundabout motion of his arm. Delicately, he touched the bandage that held the splint.

That guy has *patience*, Jeremy thought. Maybe he's using it on me, too.

McAdam had been carefully undoing the gauze. Now he gingerly touched the leg itself. The buck hardly noticed.

Must be good news, thought the boy. If something hurts, you jump.

McAdam was redoing the bandage. Jeremy waited until he was done, then started back toward the pen. There was a softness around the old guy's eyes when they met at the gate, but it was hard to tell what that meant.

"Well, I'm very glad to see that the swelling around the break has finally gone down," McAdam said. "But whether that splintered bone is going to heal properly is another question. The vet thought it would be a waste of time to do anything except finish him off. But I just couldn't go through with that—not as long as there's some reason to hope. So now we'll just have to wait a few weeks and see."

"*We?*"

McAdam smiled. "Just a way of speaking. I'm running a refuge, not a prison, Jeremy. Now you can throw most of that brush over the fence. Do it carefully and make sure you don't hit him with any of it. Then take what's left to that other pen over there, the tiny one. That's where we're going to put the fawn in a little while. What I'd like you to do is make a soft place that he can sink down on. I'll be in back of the cabin when you're through, making a new mommy for him."

"What?"

McAdam lifted a parting hand. "You'll see when you get there."

In spite of the coolness of the morning, Jeremy was sweating by the time he was finished and went to join the old guy. McAdam was using a hand drill on a dummy that was about three and a half feet tall, shaped and colored like a deer. The dummy was upside down, wedged between two sawhorses while McAdam bore holes into the chest.

Jeremy caught on. "*That's* the mommy."

"Yup. These dummies are used for bow and arrow target practice. This one is hollow and the head unscrews. If I take that off I can stick a nursing bottle all the way down inside. The tip of it will stick out through the bottom just about where one of the mother's nipples should be."

"What a lucky fawn. It's got a wooden mother."

McAdam looked up. "Better than none at all, don't you think?"

"Yeah . . . maybe," Jeremy said huskily. That weight in his chest was coming back. He tried to make his sigh so small that the man wouldn't notice it.

"Well, no, it's not a perfect answer. But it's a mistake

to let a wild creature become too attached to you when it's young, the way I did with Mitzi. This way, when I do release the fawn later on, he'll have a better reason for trying to snuggle up to a real doe than if I keep on acting like his mother. At least, that's what I'm hoping. There, I'm done! Let's test it out."

Pulling the dummy away from the sawhorses, he turned it right side up and began to take off the head. "Give me that bottle on the stump, will you, son."

He's starting again with the bit of calling me son, Jeremy told himself as he went for the bottle. Maybe *that's* why he's bribing me to stay here. Maybe this stalling me has nothing to do with that phone call last night. The guy's lonely and he thinks I'm a candidate for the job of being *his* kid. *Weird!*

"Here you go," he said extra gently, as if he was talking to someone who was soft in the head and needed to be treated just right.

McAdam gave him a strange look. "Thanks."

"You got a family, sir?"

"*Sir?* No. Not anymore. Call me Aaron." Pushing the bottle into the dummy, he started to shove his arm in behind it.

"So . . . Aaron, what happened to them?"

"My little girl was killed. And my wife and I drifted apart. That was a long time ago. Wait a minute, I'm not getting my hand down far enough."

"Give me the bottle."

"My pleasure," said McAdam, pulling his arm out.

52

Jeremy's slender hand slipped in easily, found the hole on the bottom, and nudged the nipple through. It was a simple enough thing to do, but it gave him a good feeling all the same.

"Well, I think we're in business here," said McAdam. "Can it be that the two of us are going to make a good team this morning, after all?"

"You never know."

McAdam grinned at him. "Stranger things have happened."

Jeremy was silent for a moment. "Mind if I ask you something about your daughter?"

"How she died?"

"Well, yeah."

"No, I don't mind," McAdam said very softly, and looked up at him. "A hunter shot her. A drunken fool with a gun."

Jeremy's mouth opened, closed, and opened again. "Listen, I'm real sorry."

"Thanks. So am I. Well, back to the living. Why don't you go get the fawn and bring him out here?"

"*Me*?"

"Don't worry, I've cleaned up the bathroom."

"Got a . . . got a leash or something?"

"Look son . . . Jeremy . . . just pick him up like you would a dog."

"Yeah, well, I never picked up a dog."

"Then you've missed something. Here's your chance to make up for it."

When he stepped into the bathroom, Jeremy found

the tiny creature backed behind the toilet, eyes glittering with fear as it peered at him.

Jeremy went into a crouch, figuring that if he spoke to the fawn in a gentle tone of voice it wouldn't matter what words he used. "So listen, bro," he began, "let's not make a major case out of this, okay? Here's the deal. You don't kick me or anything like that, and I don't throw up all over you. Who knows, maybe we'll have a chance at one of those heartwarming boy and his pet situations. That's fair, right? Okay, here we go."

But when he put out his arms, the fawn cringed. And when he moved in closer, it lowered its little head as if it already had antlers to fight back with.

Jeremy knew better than to blame this helpless orphan for being terrified of him, but he couldn't help having that old bad feeling of not being wanted. "I don't need this," he said, and began to turn away.

Yet how could he just walk off? What would he tell McAdam—that he let his *feelings* get hurt by some little animal? Tapping his foot three or four times, he decided to just be quiet and sit down on the floor.

While he waited Jeremy began to wonder how this baby might have gotten separated from its mother. All of the possibilities were sad, but especially the thought that she might have left her newborn child because she hadn't wanted to have one so late in the year. Or maybe because the baby was scrawny or not good-looking enough or something like that. That was worse than any accident, a mother dumping her kid just because she *wanted* to!

Jeremy knew a boy whose mom had done that. She'd just left him on the front steps of a hospital, giving no reason at all—and was he ever screwed up!

At least *that* was one thing Jeremy's mom would never pull on him. Oh, she'd do lots of other stuff, especially if Ed was around, but not that. Not a chance! The only reason they weren't together right now was that *he* had taken off, not her—and that was *different*!

Yet somehow he couldn't help thinking about the crazy thing that had happened at the supermarket—her taking Ed's dare to go in and boost a carton of cigarettes for him. Ed knew how Jeremy felt about his mother going to do a stupid kid-stuff thing like that, and she knew it, too! That's why Ed snickered at him as she walked away from the gas pump to go into the store. He didn't even have to put it into words. What he was letting him know was, *You lose, Jeremy. She takes me over you every time!*

Lost in these bitter thoughts, Jeremy's fingers had been idly tracing the cracks between the tiles on the floor. He didn't notice a stirring in the room until a little nose inched closer and closer to those fingers and began to sniff the wonderful odor of the cedar branches they had collected earlier. But Jeremy felt the barest touch of air against his skin, and looking down, he saw the fawn. The animal looked up at the same time, and when their eyes met, the fawn gave a little start. But Jeremy was so still now that the animal did not shrink back. And its gaze seemed to be asking him: *Can I trust you?*

Well, that was a question he'd been asking McAdam one way or another. And there was no way he could get an answer to really count on. Not from anybody. Not even from his own . . .

He didn't want to think about that. Especially not with this little animal in his arms. . . . Hey, wait a minute. How had that had happened? Jeremy got up and left the cabin, feeling the fawn warm against his cheek, walking slowly to make sure he didn't stumble. His own heart was racing.

McAdam didn't ask what took him so long. "Don't bring the fawn too close to the dummy," he said. "Put him down over there and let him find his mommy by himself."

"Do you know what happened to the real mother?"

"Hit by a car. I found him by the roadside. He was trying to draw milk but all the heat was gone out of her. So he must have been there a long time. No more talk now. Watch."

They waited while the fawn studied the dummy. Slowly, it became more and more curious. Finally it went over, found the nipple, and began to nurse.

"I'm going to call him either Spots or Tiny," Jeremy exclaimed.

Then he looked up. McAdam was beaming widely. Quickly, he corrected himself. "You know, for the rest of this morning."

"I understand," said McAdam. But the grin remained.

CHAPTER

After the feeding they carried the fawn and his "mother" to the baby pen. Aaron went into the larger enclosure to freshen the water in the lame deer's bucket. He came out gazing at the clear blue sky and shaking his head in disappointment. "Hoped we'd get a good rain yesterday but nothing happened. We'll have to put some more well water in the creek."

Jeremy stared at him. "We're going to *put* water in a creek?"

"Most natural place to go looking for it, don't you think?"

"Huh?"

McAdam merely held up a hand and said nothing more until they returned to the cabin. Jeremy filled three buckets in the bathtub and brought them out one by one. McAdam sealed the tops with plastic and loaded them onto the pickup. Then they drove slowly to the little wooden bridge near where Jeremy had taken his tumble the night before.

"We'll set them down there in the middle," McAdam said, indicating the bed of rocks below. Going around to the back of the pickup, he handed down the buckets and took two of them for himself.

"This stream should have been flowing by now," he explained as they lugged the buckets down the slope and left them on the dried-out creek bed. "But we've had a bad time of it since the summer drought. When they can't find water up here, the animals go farther down the mountain where it's easier for hunters to get at them. Now that hunting season's about to start . . ."

He didn't finish his sentence. Just then a red-crested head bobbed up in the bushes, then ducked down again.

"Hey, Aaron, was that a turkey?"

"Yup. It won't come out to drink until we're gone."

"There are *wild* ones?" Jeremy asked as they went back.

"Up here in the north woods. Way down south in the jungles. All over the Americas, in fact. Turkeys were even here before the Indians." He stopped beside the truck door. "So if anybody calls you a turkey, take that as a compliment. It means you're an original American."

"Yeah, right."

Jeremy went around to the passenger's side. Before he could climb in, Aaron lifted one side of the long seat up. Just beneath it was an open compartment that was mostly filled with tools. But Jeremy's attention was drawn to a closed metal box with a hand-painted skull and crossbones on the lid.

McAdam reached past it and pulled out a couple of empty rolled-up feed bags. "We're going to collect apples," he explained, putting the seat back in place. Then he started to walk away.

Jeremy had to move fast to overtake his long-legged strides toward the woods. "So what's in that box?"

"Inside my little house of horrors, you mean?" McAdam lit up with enthusiasm. "Fourth of July firecrackers like you've never seen before. I'm saving them for the first day of deer hunting season, when most of the killing is done."

He broke into a wide and mischievous grin. "Then I'm going down the deer trails ahead of the hunters and set them off!"

Jeremy gave him a warning look. "You're going to make some people steam."

"That could be."

"People carrying *loaded* guns."

"And maybe loaded themselves." McAdam was no longer grinning.

His face had clouded over so quickly that Jeremy wondered what the man was thinking about now. Maybe about that wild gunshot which had killed his daughter. "So where's Mitzi?" he asked to break the heavy mood.

McAdam brightened at once. "Why? Do you miss her?"

"No! Just wondering."

"Well, it's a good question. She usually comes down from her ledge to keep me company on my chores."

"Maybe my being around is making her jealous."

They were entering the big field now, tromping though weeds and tall grass. McAdam bent his head and began to study the ground closely. "I can use your help now, youngster. Spread out and look for Popsicles."

Jeremy pulled a face. "Oh yeah, sure. *Popsicles*."

"I'm not talking about chocolate-covered ice cream, Jeremy. This kind is on a stick, too, and pretty much the same shape, but it's made out of molasses and salt and a few other ingredients the deer go crazy over. The hunter just shoves it into the ground, then leaves it for deer to find. Once they do, they'll keep coming back to lick it. Anyone who hides in the right place long enough can hardly miss making the kill." When Jeremy frowned, he quickly added. "Doesn't sound like a real sporting way of going after an animal, does it?"

"No. But you don't have to preach at me."

"Didn't mean to."

"There ought to be a law against them."

"There is. They've been outlawed for years. So have traps. But the state can't afford to hire a lot of inspectors to enforce those laws. And even if one of the local folks is caught by one of the local officers . . . well, I guess you heard how that deputy sheriff feels about what I'm trying to—"

Jeremy cut him off suddenly. "What color are those

Popsicles?" He was squinting at a small object poking up among the weeds.

"Could be gray or brown or—"

"Right there!" he said, pointing, and started toward it.

McAdam overtook him quickly. "No, I'll get it."

The boy shook his head. "What are you worried about, Aaron?" he called after him "Booby-trapped Popsicles?"

"I know I'm probably being overcautious," McAdam called back. "But just bear with me, all right?"

Jeremy watched him pull a knife from the sheath which hung from his belt, then kneel and pick at the earth around the object. Finally satisfied that it was only what it seemed to be, he plucked it from the ground and waved the boy over. By the time Jeremy arrived, McAdam was peering at the surrounding woods through the binoculars that hung from his neck on a strap.

"See anybody?"

"No. Let's keep going."

Jeremy grew thoughtful. "You're thinking somebody might want to hurt you because you don't like hunting?"

"Yes and no. I've never been very popular around here."

"Uh-huh. Only now you've got company so you have to be real careful, right?"

McAdam gave him a sidelong glance. "How come you speak English so badly but think so clearly?"

Jeremy shrugged. "I dunno. Guess I'm lucky both ways."

Their patrol ended not far from the remains of a burned-down farmhouse, beyond which was a stand of long neglected apple trees. All that remained upright among the charred ruins was a half-collapsed stone chimney. Something lying at its base caught Jeremy's eye. Without waiting for McAdam's permission he veered over to it and brought back an opened beer can. The few drops inside were being soaked up by the crushed butt of a cigarette.

McAdam examined it and turned grim. "Now you stay here. You understand?"

"Oh, come on—"

"I mean it." Wagging a finger at him, McAdam turned and strode toward the abandoned grove. "Who's in there?" he shouted out, cupping a hand to his mouth.

No answer.

"This is posted private property and you're trespassing. But if you come out, there'll be no problem. I just want you off my land."

Still no answer.

Jeremy watched McAdam stoop just long enough to pick up a log about the size of a baseball bat and disappear among the trees. He stood there, trying to make up his mind about the sanity of the guy. First McAdam had acted like bait for a deer might be a bomb about to go off. And then, just because some slob had dropped a beer can . . .

Now he began to grow aware of stomping sounds among the wild apple trees. He took a few steps toward them, calling "Hey, Aaron? What's happening?"

"Didn't I tell you to stay away?" McAdam shouted back amid the thuds. "Do it!"

Suddenly there was a snapping, crunching sound. Then dead silence.

Forget this waiting around, Jeremy told himself. Grabbing a piece of blackened timber longer than himself, he rushed in after McAdam.

He found the man standing over a deep pile of fallen leaves and worm-eaten apples. One end of the makeshift bat was sticking straight up out of the ground by itself. Jeremy looked down and saw what was holding it. Teeth. Metal teeth as big as a shark's, set in a ring around the bat with their points buried deep in the wood.

But it wasn't this that startled him as much as the change that had come over McAdam. He was staring pop-eyed at the trap, his face turning red as fire.

"It's for bears," he began in a low rumbling tone, as if the words were coming from deep within a cave. "A steel-jaw leg trap." His voice began to rise into a cry of anguish. "Look what it would have done to Mitzi. Or to *you*! Either of us could have tripped the spring, been crippled and in agony. *Is this right? Is this right to do to any living creature?*"

"But it worked out okay," said Jeremy soothingly as he watched the corners of McAdam's mouth begin to twitch. "You did a good job."

"A good job . . . yes . . . thank you." The words seemed to calm his tremors, but only for a moment. "I don't have to live with this cruelty here!" he shouted. "Not on my own land. Not in this refuge!"

Yanking the contraption off the ground, McAdam uncovered the chain that was attached to it, traced the links to the foot of a tree, and untied the trap. Then he raced up a rise to a boulder that stood alone in the midst of the old grove. Howling with rage, he slammed the trap down on the rock with all his force.

When that hardly put a dent in the device, McAdam scrambled among the few loose and heavy rocks nearby. Lifting the biggest one all the way above his head, McAdam brought it down on the trap so hard that the rock itself shattered. But even that didn't stop him. He found another to pound with. Then another and another.

With each blow, the trap began to give way, the teeth bending. Still, the enraged man would not let up. And Jeremy, watching a face that had turned a deep purple, was afraid.

"Stop it!" he screamed.

There was enough sharpness to Jeremy's words to slice through to McAdam now. His hammering slowed. His arms came down. The rock rolled away from his fingers and the blood drained slowly from his face.

"I'm sorry," he said after drawing a few deep breaths. "It's been a long time since I went off like that and I'm very sorry you had to see it. Watching me must have scared you pretty badly."

"No big deal," Jeremy said dryly. "I've seen worse, believe me."

"Have you? Well, I want to thank you all the same. You brought me back—and you're certainly nobody's fool."

That remark would have pleased Jeremy a lot more if McAdam didn't follow it with a questioning look.

"I'm nobody's fool, right? I know you must have been listening to my phone call last night. So you're wondering how come I'm dumb enough to want to get a gun and go after Ed."

"I think that puts it pretty well."

Jeremy forced a grin. "Hey, weren't you ever a kid? Couldn't you tell it was just a *fantasy*?"

"That's all it was? A fantasy?"

"Now you got it. It made me feel better, that's all, to tell myself how I was going to go and rescue my mom by blowing the guy away. But it'll never happen."

"I can't tell you how relieved I feel."

McAdam moved to put a hand on Jeremy's shoulder, but the boy stepped away. He didn't need this buddy-buddy stuff.

"So, look," Jeremy said. "Since you know that I won't go off and blow anybody away, do I have to put any more time in before I get my twenty bucks?"

McAdam frowned. Maybe the guy was just a cheapskate, like other people Jeremy had met who would rather say you didn't need something than cough up. "Look, how about we just settle for fifteen now and I'll be on my way?" Jeremy offered.

"Let's pick up a few apples. Then I think you've earned it all. Fair enough?"

"Yeah, okay." He'd just do it fast and get this over with. But, looking up, Jeremy saw there were no apples on the branches. "Hey, Aaron, they're all on the ground and they've got black holes in them. That means worms, right? The buck's not gonna eat 'em that way, is he?"

"Whatever he won't, Mitzi will."

The apples were tiny, small enough to grab three at a time. Without coming out of a squat, Jeremy hopped with his sack from place to place, dumping them in fast. "How many of these do we need?"

"A lot. I'm going to put them out in different places tonight. The more I leave somewhere else, the more the deer will stay away from here. I've always had a bad feeling about this grove. And now with that trap . . ."

"You think the same guy who left the Popsicle put it there?"

"Probably, and I have a good idea who. I want to catch him at it."

Jeremy stared at him. "Be careful."

"Oh, I will."

"Yeah? Why is it I don't believe you?"

"Well, you should. Anyway, we're finished. So here's what I owe you." McAdam drew out a wallet and handed him two tens.

"Thanks, man."

"Wait. This is for good measure."

He held out another five, but Jeremy made no move to take it. "What's that for? Are you feeling so glad I told you I was gonna be a good boy that you wanna give me a tip?"

"Not at all. Calming me down was beyond the call of duty."

"Fine." He plucked the extra bill from McAdam's hand, shoving it into his pocket with the rest. "Still driving me to the station like you said you would?"

"Yes, I will."

"So, can we go now?"

"All right."

Leaving the grove, they started back across the open field in silence, each following the threads of his own thoughts. As they went past the pens Jeremy paused to gaze at the fawn. But it gave him a pang, and he moved on.

"So, Jeremy," McAdam said on the path to the cabin. "When you get to the city, then what? Any plans as to what you'll do? How you'll live?"

The question sunk as deeply into the boy's gut as a boxer's fist. Better to think about that later, dope it out on the way down. "That's not your problem," Jeremy said to end the conversation. But it didn't.

"I took on some of that problem when I got you away from the deputy," McAdam said with a sigh.

"Hey, listen, it was nice what you did, but with you or without you nobody would have caught me. And like I told you yesterday, I didn't ask for your help."

"You took it, though. Jeremy, I think that entitles me to make a suggestion."

"What?"

"Call your mother and just listen to what she has to

say. You might find out that your running away has made her take another hard look at what she's doing."

Jeremy's steps slowed again, but only for an instant. "Yeah, right. I'm gonna call her at his place to find out if she's gonna leave him. That makes a lot of sense."

"Maybe not, but don't you at least want her to know you're all right? And that you still love her?"

Jeremy felt the pressure of McAdam's words weighing him down. "Are you finished making suggestions yet?" he snapped.

"I suppose I'm finished."

"*Okay!* I'll call."

CHAPTER

6

When they arrived at the cabin, McAdam hung back by the door. "Maybe you'd rather not have me around while you're talking."

"It ain't my house." Jeremy paused by the phone. "Just don't get into it or do anything to give away where I am, all right?"

McAdam nodded, but that wasn't enough for Jeremy. "I want to hear you promise."

"Yes, I promise. Why don't I just make us something to eat?"

"Great. I'll never turn down food! Thanks." Jeremy waited until McAdam passed into the kitchen. Then he took a long, jittery breath and dialed Ed's number in the city.

The phone rang only once before he heard his mother's anxious "Hello."

Gulping hard, Jeremy opened his mouth. Nothing came out.

"Hello?" repeated the voice nervously. "Who is this?"

He answered so faintly that it must have been almost impossible to hear him. "It's me."

"Jeremy?"

Jeremy nodded. Then, remembering that she couldn't see him, he muttered, "Yeah."

His mother's cry of relief exploded in his ear. "Oh, thank God! Oh, my baby! You don't know . . . I can't tell you . . . Oh, I'm so happy! I'm—" And she broke into choking sobs.

Oh, sure, she's real happy, Jeremy told himself miserably. "Mom, don't cry. Please don't—"

"Darling, I didn't know what to do. I wanted to stay up there till they found you but the police said to go home and wait. I did, but I felt . . . I felt like I was deserting you. And I was so afraid I'd never see you again."

"But, Mom, that's crazy. Of course you will. You know, sometime."

"Sometime?" Her voice rose shrilly. "What do you mean *sometime*? Aren't you coming home? Didn't the police find you?"

"No."

"Where *are* you?"

"Mom, I'm okay." He couldn't tell her any more than that.

"Jeremy, please answer me! Tell me where you are!"

I gotta be strong, he said to himself. I gotta hold out. Not just for me—for her, too! "Mom, are you going to stay with him?"

"You're damn right she is!" bellowed Ed.

And now Jeremy realized that Ed was right there by the phone, staying in control of anything that went on, as usual. So nothing was going to come of this. His voice dropped into his shoes. "I gotta go, Mom."

"No!" she shouted. "Jeremy, no! *Don't hang up!*"

Even from halfway across the cabin McAdam had heard this plea. He came out of the kitchen to catch the boy's eye.

Jeremy was looking at him when his mother cried, "Please, listen to me! I understand why you ran away. Just—"

But now Ed was bellowing again. "Listen, damn it, you're only a *kid*. You don't have the right to make decisions for your mother!"

"This is between me and my mom," Jeremy shouted back. "So butt out! You put her back on the phone!"

"No! And whether you believe me or not, I've been worrying about you just like she has! But I have had it up to here with your selfishness! You don't care about anything but what *you* feel! I'm telling you right now that no matter what happens, you aren't ever gonna break up *my* home."

Where was Mom? Was she being kept away from the phone? What kind of noises were those? Jeremy could hear her pleading from a few feet away. "Ed, this is wrong. You've got to let me talk to my—"

Ed cut her off. He sounded the way he did before he'd hit her, like someone was doing terrible things to *him.*

"What's the matter with you, Corinne! Do you want a twelve-year-old jealous brat to tell you how to live? When he couldn't keep you to himself he ran away. Well, now I want him to *stay* away!"

"Ed, *please!*"

"No! The hell with this. I'm hanging up and don't you try to stop me!" There was a crashing noise, but the phone didn't go off. Other sounds followed it: glass breaking, furniture going over. From somewhere across that other room, Ed was screaming again. "You still want to talk to your son after all he's pulled? Well, fine and dandy then. You go ahead! I'm outta here."

A door slammed. There was the sound of the receiver being scraped up off a floor.

"Mom?"

He heard short, heavy breaths.

"Mom?" Jeremy repeated bitterly. "He hit you, didn't he?"

"No," she said at last in a voice that was half a moan. "We were wrestling for the phone and it dropped. That's all that happened."

"Yeah, sure."

"It *is*, I swear.

"Mom, I'm begging you to get away from him right now."

"Oh, why can't you try to understand?" she pleaded. "I never had anybody who really wanted to take care of me, whether he did it perfectly or not. I never had anybody to love me."

"But Mom, *I* love you."

"Yes, you love me, but . . ." Her voice took on the bewilderment of a little girl who had been terribly hurt. "But you also ran away from me!"

"Not from you, Mom! From *him!*"

"But we have to have faith in people we love when they say that they're going to change."

Jeremy shifted from one foot to another. "Oh, Mom, don't you realize how many times he said he was going to get help, only he never did? I can tell by your voice that even *you* don't really believe him anymore!"

"You're wrong. I *have* to believe him, Jeremy."

"Well, I don't!" he suddenly screamed. "And before he breaks your face again or kills you, I'm going to kill him!"

"Don't even talk like that," his mother gasped.

"I mean it!"

McAdam had been shaking his head. Now he said, "Son, you're scaring her to death. And what good does that do?"

"Who is that, Jeremy? Who is that man?"

Jeremy glared at McAdam and covered the phone. "You made me a promise! Now you're breaking it."

"But I have an idea," McAdam said, putting his hand out for the phone. "If you just let me talk to her maybe we can work it out so—"

Jeremy wouldn't listen anymore. He could hardly breathe. It was as if great blocks of stone were pressing down on him and he couldn't push them off.

"Good-bye, Mom!" he cried, slamming the phone

down. Then he bolted from the cabin.

McAdam called after him, but Jeremy wouldn't listen. His flying feet took him far from the voice and over the wooden bridge to the road, the sobs exploding as he ran.

Just as Jeremy got to the gorge, Mitzi burst from the bushes. She was charging straight at him, moving faster than a man could run.

Jeremy fell back. But before he could even turn and race away, she had closed most of the distance between them. Then all at once, not ten feet short of knocking him down, the bear came to a sudden and peaceful halt.

Jeremy was still catching his breath when she turned and slowly trotted off. In confusion, he watched her pause to gaze at him over her shoulder, move on, then glance back again.

"She loves to play tag," explained McAdam, jogging up behind him, panting. "She's letting you know that it's your turn. Now you're supposed to chase her till you almost catch her." McAdam planted a hand on his shoulder. "She'll be disappointed if you don't."

As if in agreement, Mitzi dipped her head.

Suddenly, without really knowing why, Jeremy started laughing. He laughed so hard his sides hurt, so hard that the tears that were still in his eyes looked like tears of laughter. That was just as well. It had been a rule for a long time that nobody would ever see him crying.

CHAPTER

Perhaps McAdam could tell that this was a special sort of laughter, the kind that came to the rescue when things were so bad a person couldn't go on without finding something hilarious to roar at.

He waited until Jeremy grew quiet, then gently began. "In your heart of hearts, I think you know that you'd be better off staying in the refuge right now than anyplace you might be running to. And for my part, I could use your help with Mitzi. She's getting a little rambunctious lately because nature is trying to get her attention, but she just doesn't want to listen."

McAdam grew silent for a moment, then added, "I apologize for breaking my promise."

Jeremy shrugged. "Everybody breaks promises."

"I take mine very seriously. It wouldn't happen again."

"Sure it would! But I know what you were trying to do for me, so it's no big deal. Let's just forget about it. Now what's this story about Mitzi?"

"She should have gotten ready for her winter sleep by now, like all the other pregnant bears. I'm afraid that if she doesn't pull a disappearing act before the hunting season starts, someone will shoot her. Mitzi has the mistaken notion that we humans are only on this earth for the purpose of being her playmates. That's my fault—I let her get too close to me for her own good. But she was only a tiny cub when she lost her mother and I couldn't find another bear to take her in. What I'd like now is for you and I to go up to the cave where I found her and spend some time there. This afternoon we'll take on the role of mama bears and show her how to get her den ready. And tonight we'll stretch out in a couple of sleeping bags in there to give her a homier feeling about the place."

Jeremy stared hard at him. "That's crazy!" he exclaimed.

"You might be right. But I don't see how anything will be lost by trying."

"Oh, sure. *I'm* gonna lie down next to a bear."

"Well, I wouldn't worry unless Mitzi rolls over in her sleep."

"That was a joke, right?" Watching McAdam come toward him, Jeremy realized he was about to have his shoulder patted or his hair mussed. Should he duck away or just stand there for it?

McAdam lightly touched his arm. "Right, son, it was just a joke. So what do you say we go collect those bedrolls and get started?"

After having someone watch him cry . . . and get scared . . . and have a crazy laughing fit . . . Jeremy needed to hang tough. He tilted his head up and asked, "Are you going to pay me for this?"

"What? After you told me the twenty dollars was a bribe?"

"I got nothing against bribes."

"Too late. This is room and board stuff."

Jeremy shuffled his feet. He had to make it clear that there was some kind of a bottom line here. "No go, unless you fix the TV."

He waited. McAdam rubbed his hands, thinking it over. "We'll see if your work is worth it."

The boy gave him a sharp look. "Oh? I haven't done good, so far?"

"That was before. This is going to be now. What do you say?"

"Okay."

Now McAdam did clap him on the shoulder. "Glad to have you back, son."

"I keep telling you, don't call me 'son.'" But Jeremy waited a few seconds before he ducked away. "Let's get the show on the road," he announced, and dashed ahead of McAdam to get the bedrolls from the cabin.

McAdam called after him to look behind a panel up in the sleeping loft. There were sweaters for him, too, and he'd find them in the . . .

But Jeremy was already out of range.

There were two panels, not one, facing Jeremy

when he climbed the ladder and crawled past the bed to the back wall. The bedrolls were behind the largest one. He tossed them over the low railing and opened the other panel to look for the sweaters. But all he found were little packets of photographs. Jeremy drew some out and saw what McAdam had looked like when he didn't have a beard and his hair was dark. And he saw the little girl and her mother.

Usually, Jeremy knew, people liked to show off their family pictures, full of loving, smiling faces. But somehow he had the feeling that he was peeking where he didn't belong, and that this was a sneaky thing to do. Shoving the photos back in place, he went down the ladder.

With all the bookshelves, plus the sofa and the two chairs in the room below, there was no space for any closets. But there was a cedar chest in a corner. Lifting the lid, Jeremy saw several neatly folded piles of sweaters. Most of them were way too big for him. But there was a fluffy woolen one he recognized from one of the snapshots. Aaron's wife had been wearing it in front of a camping tent. It fit him perfectly.

Jeremy went outside and saw McAdam pulling a collapsible shovel from a little crawl space under the feed barn. Mitzi was there too, but her eye was on Jeremy, as if she hoped that he might be coming out with a piece of pie or a Tootsie Roll.

Tossing one of the bedrolls to McAdam, Jeremy ran past Mitzi, shouting, "No treat for you yet, girl. Come on! Let's go fix your den and turn you back into a *real* bear."

But Mitzi showed no interest in cooperating in that worthy task. The higher they climbed toward the little cave under the topmost ledge of Black Mountain, the more she hung back. Eventually, she vanished altogether.

McAdam thought they should start to prepare the den anyway. He wasn't quite sure, he said, whether animals were able to have guilty feelings, but Mitzi certainly did know when he disapproved of her. She was probably moping around right now, aware that they were fixing up *her* den for *her* babies. "Eventually she'll show up," he declared.

"You hope."

McAdam sighed. "I hope." Opening his shovel, he set about removing jagged rocks from the earthen floor of the shallow cave. Jeremy had a pleasanter job— cutting fresh, sweet-smelling evergreen boughs to place in the den.

Bears, McAdam explained, don't completely hibernate during the winter the way some animals do. In later weeks Mitzi would have to wake up long enough to freshen up her den so that everything would be cozy when her cubs were born in January. He was hoping that by then she'd be ready for motherhood.

"How big are the cubs when they're born?" Jeremy asked.

"About fourteen ounces."

Jeremy stopped cutting. "*Ounces*. That's less than a pound. Even I was seven pounds when I was born."

"But it's true."

"Uh-huh. Then tell me how you can look at her and see that she's pregnant?"

"I can't. But I knew she was ready and . . ."

"And what?"

McAdam began to blush. "Why don't we drop it?"

Jeremy caught on. "You *spied* on her!" he cried in surprise.

"Not on purpose."

"I'll bet."

"Now listen—"

"Come on, come on, let's hear the excuse."

"I don't have to give an excuse," McAdam snorted. "I'd heard someone on the other side of the gorge blasting away with an automatic. I didn't know whether it was for target practice or if the shooter didn't care that July is out of season for hunting. I was standing just above here on Eagles' Roost and as usual I had my binoculars, so I started looking for signs of injured animals. Then I saw this other bear introducing himself to Mitzi."

"*Introducing?*"

McAdam glanced past him, obviously delighted to have a reason for changing the subject. "Well, well, look who's just come home. It's the lady of the house."

Mitzi lumbered in slowly, eyeing the den. Going over to the shallow hole, she pawed it once or twice, came up to the brush Jeremy was holding, and sniffed.

Then she took a little turn around the inside of the cave to finish her inspection, lifted her nose, and walked out.

"Talk about stuck-up!" Jeremy burst into laughter, but it only lasted for a moment or two. Something else was welling up inside of him, something that caused his eyes to blink and made it hard to swallow. Something that had been there all along.

"You're worrying about your mother," McAdam guessed out loud.

"Yeah. Maybe I better call her. Just so she understands, you know, that I love her."

"I think that's a very good idea. Want me to come with you?"

"No."

"Well, since you're going down and it's getting near time to feed the fawn—"

"Formula's in the fridge. Already mixed, right?"

"Yes. You just—"

"It's covered." Jeremy started down the slope.

"Also, Jeremy, change the water and put more cedar brush in the big pen."

Jeremy stopped. "Anything else, Master?"

McAdam chuckled. "They'll never catch anybody being *your* master."

"Long as you know it." He started off again.

"Actually, Jeremy, you might try giving him half a scoop of cracked corn. In a few weeks he'll refuse it and start eating tree bark. But right now I think the weather is still warm enough for his system to digest it."

"You going to let me go now or what?"

"Sure." But McAdam quickly had an afterthought. "Hold on a minute," he called. "Make sure you memorize some landmarks on your way down. Otherwise you could have a problem coming back. It gets dark very quickly around here."

"I'll manage."

"There's a flashlight on the counter in the—"

"I can just about handle your being like a father to me," Jeremy snapped. "You don't have to be a mother, too!" Silence fell behind him at last.

After a while the slope leveled off a bit. The thick oaks and maples and the tall, curving white birches gave way to the twisted branches of that overgrown apple orchard he'd been to before. Immediately, Jeremy sensed that some change had taken place there since this morning.

As he walked along, Jeremy could find no reason for this uneasy feeling. He was about to leave the grove when he caught a faint whiff of cigarette smoke behind him on the right. He turned quickly, but there was no one to see.

Jeremy found himself staring up at the boulder where McAdam had pounded the bear trap. They had left it there twisted and bent. But now . . .

The trap was gone.

Jeremy felt so spooked he was glad to be leaving the trees for the open field. But as he walked past the farmhouse ruins, he smelled that burning cigarette.

Again he saw no one, heard nothing. There was no place among the burned and rotting timbers for anyone to crouch behind. But there *was* the old stone chimney that was still partly standing . . .

Jeremy stopped breathing as the hairy hand of an unseen man rose above it, holding a can of beer. "Here I am, kid!" said a slurred voice. "Come on over and say hello."

That was the last thing Jeremy wanted to do. Then he caught the glint of a gun barrel poking up from behind the chimney.

Chill, Jeremy ordered himself, trying to recall the time he'd kidded some gangbangers out of carving him up with a machete. Don't panic.

"Sure man, why not?" Jeremy called back, slipping his hands into his pockets and putting an easygoing swing into his walk. But when he saw the fellow sitting there, Jeremy's mouth fell open.

It was as if he was looking at Ed.

CHAPTER 8

The eerie thing was that the two men didn't look at all alike. Ed was skinny and longhaired, with darting eyes, and he always seemed about to jump out of his skin. But this square-headed man with his close-cut hair and powerful body seemed as solid as the mountain. His rifle, with its telescopic sights, was propped against the chimney stones on one side of him. A half-emptied six-pack and a sack with some objects in it rested beside him on the other. And lying in his lap with its jagged mouth gaping open like a wounded prehistoric pet was the mangled bear trap.

"You look thirsty," the man said. "Want some?"

"No, that's okay. Thanks anyway."

The man's face darkened slightly. "You don't like beer?"

This kind of testing was bad news. The guy was looking to turn mean. "Beer, yeah," Jeremy answered slowly. "Budweiser, no."

The creases in the man's forehead grew deeper and his eyebrows lifted. "You don't like *Bud*?"

"Not since I was six."

His remark broke the mood. The man lifted his can in a little toast to the boy before taking another slurp. "You started early, kid."

"Yeah, well, there was a guy pushing hard to make a man out of me. So, uh, I'm . . . Jason. Who are you?"

"Albert. You visiting the old fart?"

"He's . . . my uncle. And he's okay."

"That so?"

"Yeah." Jeremy looked at him steadily.

"Tough kid, eh? Good for you. I like that." His glazed eyes traveled to the hunting knife in the sheath on Jeremy's belt. "Say, that's a nice looking handle. Lemme get the feel of that thing." He held out his free hand.

Jeremy swallowed hard. "Can't. This is my protection."

"What? Against me?" Albert set the can on the ground and took a hard puff on the cigarette that had been burning down between his fingers.

"I don't know you."

"I can tell you're from the city, kid. In the country, we're a whole lot friendlier with strangers."

He smiled, but it was a cold one. Jeremy made a sudden calculation. "Okay," he said, and handed over the knife.

Hefting it, the man pointed to a thin branch, drew his arm back, and threw. He missed. "Well, this ain't my first six-pack," he growled. "Otherwise, I hit what I aim at."

"Happens," declared Jeremy, moving toward the knife. He picked it up, intending to give a breezy "so long" and walk slowly away. But those watchful eyes were making him think that would be a mistake. He returned with the knife, offering it handle first. "Try again, Al."

"It's Albert."

"Okay, Albert."

"Naw, that's okay. Hold onto it, in case I turn mean."

As he was speaking, Albert lit a new cigarette with the burning end of the old one and flicked the butt away. A withered leaf on the ground started smoldering instantly, then burst into flame.

"You hardly ever see a drought like this up in these mountains past September," said the man, stamping out the fire. "There's always plenty of rain after that to make up for the dry season. But this year's been bad in every way. You name it, and it's gone wrong. First the auto parts factory closed down and then the one making those high-speed minifans. The farmers had a rotten time of it with their corn, everything dead on the stalks."

He paused to open another beer can. "So now, finally, the deer season's coming on. That means business around here for anybody with a room to rent to some tourist who thinks he's Daniel Boone with a gun. That money will help cover expenses for the winter. But your uncle, now, his dream is to get the law to put a stop to that. See, he don't worry much about folks going broke. He's got his money socked away from years ago. And the biggest joke of it is, he doesn't even come from around here. But this is exactly where I come from. I mean, I was born in this house."

"Really?" Jeremy asked politely.

"This here house was built by a Stroud way back when the Dutch still had New Amsterdam. The first of us followed the Indian trails to get up and down the mountain. We hunted on those trails, too. Indians found them first by following where the deer were browsing. Deer are very dumb animals, kid. Come winter they'll go down the same snowy paths over and over looking for something to eat. When the food's gone, they go hungry rather than look someplace else. Don't let anybody tell you that hunting ain't a merciful act. The more deer we kill before the deep snows come, the less there are to starve to death. But Aaron McAdam now, his heart bleeds for all the Bambis in the forest!"

Albert threw a hard and sudden glance at the boy. "I'm boring you, huh? You don't like being stuck here listening to me."

"You're wrong. I'm interested."

Albert Stroud paused to let a stream of smoke out of his nostrils. "You know the road that goes down this side of the gorge? It was Strouds who built it long ago for hauling timber to the sawmill. When the snows came, though, everything turned to ice and was blocked up till

April. My great-grandmother took sick and they had to bring her down tied onto a sled. She died before they got her to the doctor in Medford. That's how it was."

"Hard but okay, right?"

"You making fun of me?"

"No. I'm just wondering how come your family didn't stay here."

"Taxes!" Stroud spat on the ground. "I was in the army, stationed in Germany, when the state sold it for back taxes."

"So my uncle bought the land from the state?"

"McAdam didn't have it then. He got it later off an old lady." Stroud reached for another beer. "She was kind of a hermit, like your uncle, but okay. She never stopped anyone from coming around here to hunt. Never posted No Trespassing and No Hunting signs on damn near every tree. Never hired a lawyer to keep anybody from even crossing the land to hunt somewhere else! And even if she had, she'd never have done that to a Stroud! But your uncle, now . . . The year before last he hauled me into court and got a judge to say I can't even come out here anymore!"

"What if I talk to him?"

"You?"

"Yeah. Why not?"

"And ask him what? To let me hunt?"

"No, to visit the place 'cause you grew up here."

"Lemme tell you something. I don't want and I don't need his permission for anything."

"All right, I see where you're coming from. Maybe I'll just stay out of it, you know?" Jeremy glanced down. "That is one big trap. Where do you buy a thing like that?"

"Hard to say. This here looks like a real old one. Has to be. They've been outlawed a long time." He gave a slanted grin. "But you look like you think it's mine. No, you wouldn't catch me breaking the law. I just found it here. Don't believe me, huh?"

Jeremy grinned back. "Can't think of anything you'd say right now I wouldn't agree with."

Stroud's free hand went out to the rifle. "Bet you're thinking I was going to use this to finish off some half-dead animal I caught."

"Not thinking anything."

"Sure, kid. But if I *was* the trapper, how would I go about it?"

Jeremy felt his stomach tighten as the man got up and slowly began to circle him.

"No, stand there a minute, kid. Don't turn with me."

Jeremy forced himself to stay still.

"You go behind it like this . . . and . . ."

Cold gunmetal pressed against the nape of Jeremy's neck. He blinked, panicked, thought of going for the knife . . . and gave it up.

"Feel it right in there, kid?"

"Yeah." The guy's only playing with me, he told himself.

"That's where you want to hit it. One shot, no fuss.

Of course a trapper wouldn't get in this close for anything but small game. With a bear, you'd want to stay a good enough distance off so it couldn't swing out at you. But here's the place you go for. Got it?"

"Got it." Jeremy waited for the gun to be pulled away, but that wasn't happening. Keep talking! he ordered himself. "Why not shoot between the eyes?"

"Because if the head's going to be hung on a wall you don't want a big hole in it."

The muzzle was still pressing into him. Stroud's voice had grown dark again. "You must be pretty tight with your uncle, huh?"

"We . . . uh . . . get along. Kind of." *Talk about something else!* "So, uh . . . that's what a trapper would to do with the bear? Mount it?"

"Well, a trapper's a businessmen. He'd find a customer for the head, I suppose. He'd cut off the paws, too, maybe, and rip out the gall bladder. That stuff brings a lot of money out in Asia. They grind it up and use it to make a special kind of medicine."

Jeremy swallowed hard and finally took the plunge. "Hey, mister, you gonna mount *my* head, or what?"

"Me? Oh. Sorry." Stroud stepped back, lowering the gun. "Got carried away there."

"Yeah, I know somebody else like that."

Stroud looked at him. "You don't scare easy, do you?"

Jeremy shrugged. "Hey, I can see you're a nice guy."

"How old are you, fourteen?"

Jeremy liked that. He came close to smiling. "Twelve."

"Bet you've been running with a street gang though, huh?"

"No, I just run with myself. Speaking of which, it was nice to meet you but I gotta be going."

"How long you staying?"

"It depends on a call I gotta make."

"You ever feel like it, come over to the Sportsmen's Lodge." Stroud jerked a finger behind him. "Trail back that way'll lead you where the sides of the gorge come together. You can't miss the place. It's just over the little iron bridge. I'm caretaking there now. We'll do some hunting."

"Cool."

"Give my regards to your uncle. Tell him I was trespassing again. Maybe I'll see you in court when you talk against me to the judge, huh?"

"Don't worry about it."

"I won't. You know why, you little city rat? Everybody around here hates McAdam's guts almost as much as I do. And now they're all real sorry that when my dad needed their help they let him down. They didn't do one damn thing to keep this place from being sold out from under my family!"

"But my uncle wasn't even around then, right? It was some woman bought it all first. That's what you told me."

"What about it?"

"Then he couldn't have anything to do with cheating your family out of this place."

"Kid, let me tell you something. When I got out of

the service I came out here and said, 'Mr. McAdam, this property was our home for over three hundred years. The Strouds are buried all over this land. I've got a little money saved up for a down payment. Will you sell it back to me?' You think he listened?"

"I know how you feel, but he must have figured by then that this was *his* home."

"Well, I got news for him. You go tell him that Albert Stroud is through waiting around to get his rights!"

"Okay, I will. So like I said before, I gotta go." He started to leave.

"Hey, kid!"

Jeremy turned around. "Yeah?"

"Didn't mean to call you names. All that was just me sounding off. I get this way sometimes." Pulling the lid off another can, he lifted it in a toast. "Forget I said a thing."

"Sure."

Freed at last, Jeremy crossed the open field to the shortcut just beyond the pens. Then he headed through trees till he saw Aaron's clearing. But the closer he drew to the cabin, the slower were his steps. The danger he'd left behind didn't trouble him nearly as much as whatever he might learn or hear when he made his phone call.

But first things first. He'd promised to feed the fawn. Going inside, he avoided even looking at the phone, and went straight to the kitchen. He took the formula from the refrigerator, warmed it on the stove to room temperature, poured it in a clean nursing bottle, put the nipple on it, and set off for the baby pen.

The fawn was sucking away at the nipple of his "mother" that had long since gone dry. When Jeremy reached down inside the dummy to remove the empty bottle, the fawn began to bleat. But as soon as he replaced it with the new one, an eager mouth closed around it and began to suckle. Those contented sounds brought peace to Jeremy as well. Kneeling beside the baby, he began to stroke its soft, warm coat.

He stayed there for several minutes, but the deer in the big pen had needs of its own. Carting in the filled bucket he'd brought with him, he removed the empty one, dragged in more bushes, and gave the buck apples and cracked corn. Then, unable to find another reason to put off calling his mother, Jeremy trudged back to the cabin.

CHAPTER

9

Several hours passed before Jeremy climbed back through the darkness to the den. He found Aaron still wide awake, but in his sleeping bag with his arms making a pillow behind his head.

"That light's shining in my eyes."

"Sorry." Jeremy snapped his flashlight off.

"Me, too, if I just sounded a little sharp with you. That happens when I worry."

"Nothing to worry about," Jeremy said glumly.

"I can see that now. But when I was lying here, I kept wondering if you'd decided to leave again. Glad you didn't. What took all this time? Did you have a problem finding the way back?"

"I don't get lost," Jeremy said, slipping into his own bag. "The phone was off. Now it's back on, okay? Good night." He turned away.

McAdam propped himself up on an elbow. "Jeremy, I'm sorry but I can't leave it like this. What are you talking about?"

"It's simple enough! Ed rips the phone out when he beats her. He pulls it out of the wall so she can't call anybody. Then when it's kissy-kissy again he reconnects it. That's the only talent he has—busting things and putting them back together again!"

"Did you talk to your mother?"

"If you can call it that, yeah. That's what I waited for. We talked."

"Was she . . . was she badly hurt?"

"I don't know! You think she'd tell me? I'm the enemy now. I called the cops!"

"Did the police go there?"

"That's how the phone got back on."

"And?"

"Well, it was all a mistake. In fact, everything was so wonderful, the cops left without doing a thing."

"What did your mother say?"

"I don't know. It was all mixed up. She didn't ask anything about where I am or what I'm doing or any of that. Instead she starts telling me that she's been thinking about how mean all those different foster home people used to be. For years she's been trying to forgive one old couple who never gave her anything. Well, they'd give her just one gift every Christmas, but then when they'd get mad at her, they'd take it away! And then she says how I was the biggest gift she ever had, and she'd thought it was for forever until I cut out on her. And then she says: 'You better stop trying to tell me that you really love me be-be-because now you can go to hell!'"

He began to blink.

"Jeremy, I'm sure she didn't really mean that."

"Oh, yeah? You wanna bet that she thinks she's got only one person left? Ed, the face smasher! Isn't that terrific?"

Jeremy wouldn't speak until he was sure he could keep anything that remotely sounded like crying from entering his voice. These were going to be facts, that's all. He was just telling Aaron the facts!

"You know . . . you know why she thinks that Ed is so wonderful? The very first day they met he gave her an engagement ring that he *said* was his mother's. But she lost it, and that's why she thinks things got so awful between them. But tonight, after the cops left, Ed went out to get her a new one. Only just as I was calling, she was down on the floor, crawling around under the bed, and she found it. And what a good sign *that* was! Only now she didn't know what to do if he came back with another ring. I'm telling you, man, it's nuts. It's all nuts."

"She wants to be with him, Jeremy."

"Look, I don't want to talk about it anymore, okay?"

"I understand."

"I don't want to talk about anything!"

"All right."

But then Jeremy blurted, "I just can't be around that kind of thing anymore. You know what I'm saying?"

"Yes, I know."

"It's no way to live!"

"I agree with you there."

The cave grew quiet. Finally, Aaron said, "There's a part of me that keeps asking why I've been letting myself get involved in all this. I suppose that's not news to you, is it?"

Jeremy didn't answer. Here it was. The kiss-off.

"But now I feel strongly that we're going to have to do something to keep you here."

Yeah, sure, Jeremy thought. Lots of luck. All the same, he felt a rush of tenderness for this man who'd been showing him so much patience and kindness.

"Thanks," he mumbled. He wondered whether to mention running into the guy who'd set the bear trap, and how dangerous Stroud seemed to be. But why get Aaron all worked up when there was nothing he could do about it now?

Thinking about Albert Stroud brought back the mystery of why that man had reminded him so much of Ed. Suddenly, the answer came to him. Each of them wore a look on his face that said as loudly as if he'd been screaming it:

"Everything wrong in my life is somebody else's fault!"

"Where's Mitzi?" Jeremy asked, to shake off these thoughts.

"Up in that tree over there, feeling cornered, I guess."

"So it's not working?"

98

"Give it a while. Everything takes time."

"Yeah. I guess you're right." He paused, and then he said guiltily, "I saw pictures of your family when I went looking for this sweater. I mean, I looked into the envelope, and I'm sorry."

"That's all right. I've got other pictures of them in my pocket—want to see them?"

"It's dark now. Maybe tomorrow."

"Sure."

Jeremy lay back. "I'm kind of surprised you don't just want to forget."

"I couldn't forget the bad memories, anyway, so I might as well keep the good ones close to me."

"Were you there when your daughter was killed?"

"There? Well, yes, right on the spot," McAdam said, with a crack in his voice. "I was the drunk with a gun who shot her."

"Oh, no!"

There was a long silence. Finally, McAdam said, "That's what I kept saying over and over for a long time afterward. But there comes a time when you just stop repeating that to yourself. Some things just can never be undone, so you go on. Do you know what I mean, Jeremy?"

"I guess so."

"Good night, then."

" 'Night."

It was chilly in the morning. Jeremy could see his breath when he crawled out of the sleeping bag and began to roll it up. McAdam was already on his feet, his own bag tied and under his arm.

"Morning, youngster. Soon as you're ready, let's go down to the pens and feed our deer."

Mitzi, who had been peacefully asleep in her tree, opened her eyes as they were breaking camp. She stretched and started to rise, but McAdam wagged a finger at her. "You stay, bad girl!"

Her head sagged. She sank down again and looked on forlornly while they went off without her.

"Think that'll do any good?" a doubtful Jeremy asked as they began the steep descent from the cave under Eagles' Roost.

"Not really." McAdam sighed. "I don't know what to do, frankly. I'm beginning to suspect that whoever set that bear trap was purposely trying to get at me by harming her."

"Your *whoever*," blurted Jeremy after a moment's hesitation, "is a character named Albert Stroud. He was down there with it last night. Said he's a caretaker at the Sportsmen's Lodge."

McAdam stopped in his tracks. "Why didn't you tell me right away?" he demanded.

The boy kept moving. "Because it was late. And I didn't want you to get red in the face again, especially when there was nothing you could do about him. And you know, there were other things on my mind just then."

"You're right. I'm sorry." McAdam followed after him. "So the man was drunk?"

"Yeah."

"What did he say?"

Jeremy had been wondering how much he ought to keep to himself. "Let me just tell you what I know, okay?"

"Go on."

"He hates you. And I've seen guys like that before. The man's gonna find a way to do something about it."

"Did he threaten *you*, Jeremy?" McAdam overtook him and turned to study the boy's face. "Did he frighten you?"

"What? You think I'm running to you? Don't worry, I handled it. But the guy was half-loaded on beer, so he talked. And he laid down a real bad rap about you."

"My problems with him go way back. And there are plenty of other people in this part of the Catskills who are against me. I'm not very well loved around here, Jeremy."

"No kidding."

"Did he actually admit to you he'd put the trap there?"

"No. He played a game about it."

"What game?"

Jeremy changed the subject. "He says shooting some deer is keeping the rest of them from starving when there isn't enough food to go around."

"How?" demanded McAdam indignantly. "By picking off the biggest, strongest males—the very ones most suited to survive? And by shooting down the mothers while they're out finding food for their little ones? Tell me, Jeremy, is that a method you would pick to control the overpopulation of human beings?"

"No, but he says deer are really dumb animals. If they weren't, they'd know how to take care of themselves better."

"They survived well enough before we crowded them out of most of their living space, just as we've done with so many other species."

"Hey, I don't want to argue with you," said Jeremy. "I'm only trying to say that people have been hunting for their food for a long, long, time."

"That's true. But now, in the present day, most hunting is just to go out and feel like a man by killing something, Jeremy. And the guns they have today can shoot enormous distances in crowded spaces. That's what has gotten me into trouble with the neighbors. In just three hours last Thanksgiving Day some visiting hunter mistook a cow for a deer, and another one sent a bullet crashing through the kindergarten window at the grade school. I went to court to stop any hunting within seven miles of the village. I wanted there to be a margin of safety from careless types who paid no attention to trail markings, hadn't the slightest idea where they were wandering to, or even what they were shooting at. But not even the superintendent of schools or the farmer who lost his cow came out to support me. There were just too many people who would lose money around here. And no one wanted to make enemies."

"Well, you've got a bad enemy coming around who thinks you don't belong on your land and that he does."

"Yes," McAdam said fretfully as they came within sight of the pens. "And it makes me worried about having you live here with me."

"Oh, I see. As soon as you get angry with me, then everything is off!"

"But I'm not angry with you. I'm glad that you have a mind of your own and you debate things. Jeremy, you misunderstand—"

"Yeah, sure I do."

"No, I mean it," said McAdam, moving in closer.

"Take your hand off my shoulder!"

But just as Jeremy ducked away, the rapid crackle of bullets jolted them both. "Down!" McAdam screamed. He pushed the boy to the ground and threw himself on top of him.

CHAPTER 10

Jeremy had been knocked breathless from the fall, but he wasn't aware of being unable to breathe as long as the firing was going on. He lay there with his fingernails clutching the dirt as if the earth itself might bring him safety.

When the shooting ended, he tried to move, but he couldn't. McAdam was sprawled on top of him, as heavy and unmoving as a stone. One thought roared through Jeremy's brain:

He's dead!

Grief for the man struck him first, terrible grief. And then horror over being pinned beneath a corpse.

Then the air stirred next to his right ear. "I'm all right. Lie still. He may be watching."

Relief filled the boy's mind. When McAdam finally started to get up, it was with a warning for Jeremy not to move. Out of the corner of his eye, Jeremy saw how carefully the man rose to his feet. McAdam was still using his own body to shield him from the gunman.

No rifle cracked, no bullet whizzed by. "All right," said McAdam at last, and he began studying the woods through his binoculars.

Jeremy rolled over into a sitting position. He still felt safer closer to the ground. "You see anyone?"

The answer came after McAdam had finished scanning the trees on the far side of the field. "No. And I wouldn't expect to, now."

"Then what are you looking at?"

McAdam pointed his binoculars higher. "For a hunter's platform in one of the branches. I should have knocked it down a long time ago. If the shots came from there, then I'm not so sure he was even aiming at us."

McAdam's voice fell to a mumble, as if he were talking more to himself than to the boy. "With a good scope on his rifle he could easily have hit us. But why risk a murder charge when there are other ways to . . ." He spun around, his gaze traveling to the animal pens a few hundred feet away.

Jeremy understood at once. "The *fawn!*"

He sprang to his feet and covered half the distance before Aaron had so much as taken a step. Through the riddled fence he saw the buck on its back, drenched in blood and jerking in its death throes. That sight brought Jeremy to a dead stop. He dreaded moving on to the smaller pen.

Yet he could see that inside that smaller space there was even more havoc. The little rain shed had splintered holes everywhere, and part of it had collapsed. But it was the toppled dummy that drew him closer to the riddled chicken wire fence. The "mother" deer no longer had a head. Its shattered body had fallen over and lay in pieces. But where was the fawn?

Already without hope, he shoved the gate open and went inside. At first the loud drumming of his own heart kept him from hearing a soft and familiar sucking noise coming from under the debris of the shed. Jeremy fell to his knees, clearing away the fallen boards until he came upon the nursing bottle. It was empty, the head broken off. Jeremy dug deeper until he found a small, thin piece of the mother's underside. The head of the bottle was still buried in it. On the other side of the fragment was the fawn. It lay there unhurt, nestled in the debris, still sucking at the rubbery nipple for the milk that would not come. Two pair of glistening eyes met each other, and Jeremy gathered the baby into his arms.

His tears were flowing now, in silence as always. But he didn't try to hide them when he heard McAdam coming up. Then the man touched his shoulder . . . and the sounds came too. These were the sobs that Jeremy had never allowed himself to hear. Not for years and years—unless you counted that one time when his mother was taken to the hospital.

Those, however, had been sobs of unhappiness. But these belonged to that place in the heart from which gratitude came.

❧   ❧   ❧

Jeremy hadn't noticed McAdam hurrying toward the cabin. But when he heard a sharp snap, he looked up and saw him loading shells into a shotgun. Jeremy jumped up, the fawn in his arms. "What's that for?"

The answer came in a choked and shaky voice as McAdam headed for the big pen. "The buck won't let go of life, Jeremy. He's suffering badly. I don't want you to be here for this."

"Wait a minute!" Jeremy shouted, rushing to cut him off at the gate. "Can't we call an animal doctor?"

McAdam stopped in front of him, his eyes a wild mixture of misery and rage. "Yes, we could. And if we were very lucky he'd come in a couple of hours or so. As soon as he got here he'd say, 'Mr. McAdam, here's another example of your softheartedness causing more pain. This deer can't be saved and you should have put him out of his agony before you called me!' That's what he'd say, Jeremy. All I can do now is finish the murderer's job for him. But I don't want you to stay for this."

He started to go around the boy, but Jeremy set the fawn down quickly and barred the way. "You don't have to. Give me the gun and I'll do it." His hand shot forward.

McAdam stared."*You*? Why?"

"It won't bother me the same way as you. I didn't take care of him all this time."

"Are you afraid I'll fall apart?"

"I didn't say that, but . . ." His voice trailed off, and

he shrugged. "I just don't want you to have it in your head later that you did it."

"That touches me, Jeremy. And I thank you for it." McAdam's voice grew deeper. He seemed steady now. "But I'm going to be all right, I promise. I've seen a lot of death and killing in my life."

"Hey, you think I haven't?" Jeremy shot back. "Seen it once in the park, only I wasn't up close. That was a stabbing. The other time was in a schoolyard in the Bronx. A kid from eighth grade came after his little brother's homeroom teacher with a gun. And I watched—"

"Stop it!" McAdam cut him off. "You recite that almost proudly."

"Ain't proud of it. It's just a fact that I took it."

"*Nobody* takes it, Jeremy. Nobody. It tears up something inside."

"Yeah, well, I can still handle it."

"This is one you won't have to. Take the fawn to the cabin. Please."

"Not a chance. At least I'm staying here with you."

"I don't often give an order. But when I do . . ."

"Okay."

Secretly relieved, Jeremy scooped up the fawn and took the shortcut through the trees.The farther he got from the pens the faster he started to go. Fifty yards from the cabin door he broke into a run, dashing into the kitchen, where he flung himself at the radio, turning it on full blast. The fawn gave a start and quivered in his arms. He covered its ears while he filled his own with blaring music.

And yet, something in him could not help listening for that shot. Something *wanted* to hear it. Jeremy winced when it came, though it was barely a pop. He tried to imagine that it wasn't the deer who had been killed out there, but Ed.

Yeah, and he himself had pulled the trigger!

But the fawn was squirming and uncomfortable. Shutting off the radio, Jeremy buried his face in its fur until he was able to drive away all thoughts except those of preparing the baby's formula.

But while he fed the baby, Jeremy's thoughts returned to McAdam and what he must be feeling. He needed to come up with the right words to help the man get over killing the buck. He could point out that the deer wouldn't have stayed alive this long if McAdam hadn't fixed its leg and taken such good care of it. And he'd done that even after the buck kicked him in the ribs!

That reminded Jeremy that he'd been giving the man some hard times in his own way. Maybe Jeremy could find a way to let the man know how he felt about him too. As long as he didn't get all mushy about it. He could say that if it had been Ed out there when the bullets were flying, there was no way he would have used his own body like a shield to keep Jeremy safe. Ed would have pulled Jeremy down on top of *him*!

Where was McAdam, anyway? He probably just

wanted to be by himself for awhile. Well, then maybe it was better to leave him alone for now.

Jeremy stretched, listening to the crackling noises in his back. Must be from lying in that cave, he told himself. Spending all that time inside a garbage can the day before didn't help any either.

Now he yawned. He'd always thought that naps were only for little kids, but a short one right now wouldn't be so bad.

He gazed down at Spots and saw that the fawn had nodded off, still sucking in its sleep. Jeremy felt the warmth of that contented little body against his own. His hand stopped stroking. His eyelids drooped, then closed.

But the sleep that overtook him would not have been as restful had he guessed what had happened to McAdam.

CHAPTER

The shotgun slug McAdam fired into the buck did something to him as well. Recoiling from the blast, he staggered back, then turned and flew into action.

Crossing the open field with the long, quick strides of someone half his age, McAdam plunged into the woods on the other side, heading for the tree platform. There was no need to come up on it from behind, for the shooter would have disappeared by now. Slinging his arm through the gun strap to free his hands, McAdam climbed the footholds that had been hammered into the trunk.

As he rose to eye level, McAdam saw at once that there were no empty cartridges lying on the deck. There had been none on the ground below, either. If the shots had indeed been fired from here, then the shooter had been careful to leave no evidence behind to take to the police.

Climbing the remaining pegs to the platform,

McAdam began examining its rough wooden boards. There was a damp spot like the splatter of a drop of water, darkening the edge facing the field. Kneeling, he put his nose close to it.

Beer. And not freshly spilt, but *stale*. The shooter must have been perched here for hours, waiting for Aaron McAdam to show up—and step just into the line of fire—before blasting away at the pens! But the gunman must have seen Jeremy as well. So it hadn't been enough punishment to leave McAdam helpless while pouring death into the pens of animals he'd been trying to save. Oh, no. The fellow had deliberately put a *child* in fear for his life.

McAdam knew well who that fellow was. Albert Stroud. He thought of what Jeremy had told him. Stroud, drunk and in the preserve last night. Stroud, who couldn't hold down a job, "caretaking" at the lodge. Yes, it had to be Stroud. But McAdam was what he had really come to take care of.

McAdam's face grew hot with frustration. So far there was no evidence to connect Stroud or anyone else to the shooting. But even if he could find some, who in the sheriff's department would do anything more than drag his feet? And even if forced to act, what would they arrest the man for? Killing a deer out of season? Damage to the pens? Trespass and mischief? It was ridiculous!

McAdam's hands clenched and unclenched by themselves, as if they were demanding to take action on their own. How he longed to find that inhuman man and let his hands take over and drive Albert Stroud down into the ground!

But what lesson would that be for Jeremy? No, he couldn't give in to this feeling. There had to be some better way. If only he could think of it. . . .

McAdam was just about to climb down from the platform when he spotted Mitzi in the distance. She was across the field, just emerging from the orchard. Finished with her unhurried breakfast of wild apples, the bear was taking her normal route toward the pens. As usual, the abandoned farmhouse was of no interest to her. But after going a few paces beyond it she stopped, lifted her head, and sniffed the air, smelling something that made her stare at the woods on this side of the field. At first, McAdam thought that she was looking for him. But no, the wind was blowing the wrong way for the air to carry his scent to her.

Snapping up his binoculars, he saw something glittering among the trees farther down—a mirror perhaps, or a strip of silver foil being rattled in the sunlight. He heard a man's distant voice shouting to the bear.

Mitzi responded. No longer just mildly nosy, she was speeding up. She was going into her charge. It was clear to McAdam that she thought she'd found a playmate for her favorite game of tag.

"Mitzi, *no!*" McAdam bellowed. But the wind only blew his voice back at him. There were an extra couple of shotgun slugs in his back pocket. McAdam fumbled for one, found it, and slammed the cartridge into the chamber. He lifted the gun and fired his warning.

Mitzi stopped, but only to listen. Unlike animals that were truly wild, she would not take alarm at gunfire or sharp sounds she did not understand. McAdam waved frantically to get her attention so he could draw her away. But before she'd even turned her head in the direction of the noise, the hunter fired.

The first bullet must have killed Mitzi instantly, for she dropped to the ground. The hunter came out of the woods, firing as he went. He didn't stop until he was standing over the slain animal. Then, taking one look at the platform where McAdam stood trembling like a man clutching a high-voltage electric wire, Albert Stroud raised his rifle high, let out a scream of victory . . . and began stamping and whooping around the body—and *on* it.

"Hey, bear lover!" he yelled, when McAdam scrambled down from the platform and came after him on the run. He began to kick the lifeless body. "Here's something for you to remember!"

In his growing madness, McAdam took aim as he ran. But Mitzi's killer only laughed. He was too far away to be within effective shotgun range. Waiting until McAdam was almost close enough to hit him, Stroud darted back into the woods and disappeared.

A new game had begun.

The game led McAdam deep into the woods. He veered this way and that, in search of a broken twig, a dented pile of fallen leaves, any sign that would lead him to his prey.

Yet there would be nothing until Stroud himself called from somewhere, taunting him, telling him that the little city rat who was staying with him would be next to die.

"But they'll put *you* away for it, McAdam! They'll say you went crazy again, like the time you had to be strapped into a straitjacket after you bagged your own kid. You think we all don't know about it because it happened way up in the Minnesota woods? Folks around here know everything about you, McAdam. You got a fan club, you might say."

McAdam would lunge after the voice and lose him again. But a cold rage was beginning to replace McAdam's wild madness, a dark state of mind where a man might still be intent upon killing, but he could now think cleverly about it. And with the rage came a realization about this cat-and-mouse game. Stroud was carefully leading him away from the wildlife preserve to Devil's Neck.

Devil's Neck was the place where the cliffs on both sides of the gorge bulged out to within less than four feet of each other before spreading apart again. A metal bridge crossed that gap, and on the other side was the Sportmen's Lodge. Stroud would be waiting for him to leave his own property and come after him there. Then if he shot McAdam, he could claim it was in self-defense and produce McAdam's shotgun as proof. After all, no one could prove it was Stroud who had riddled the pens and shot the bear. Maybe McAdam had set all that up himself. Wasn't this the same crazy man who'd been finding one reason after another to wage his own war against people's God-given right to hunt?

McAdam grew cautious as he drew near the tiny iron bridge. There was bound to be noise as he crossed those flat metal plates. It was the perfect spot for an ambush; Stroud would be a fool not to be laying in wait for him right there. And Stroud, he knew, was not a fool.

Then McAdam saw there was another way to cross the gorge. Less than five feet below the cliff there was another ledge. It was very narrow, but if he were to climb down and reach out carefully for the thick bushes overhanging the other side, he could pull himself across.

He'd have to watch his footing, though. A mixture of small leaves, pebbles, and sticks had collected in a heap on top of the jutting rock. McAdam carefully lowered his left foot, found a firm place, and bought his weight down on it. Then he brought down his right—

By the time he heard the click, it was too late. The springing steel teeth of the hidden trap punched through the thick leather of his boot, ripped the sock, and sank themselves into Aaron McAdam's flesh.

Jeremy awoke with a start. What had jarred him out of his sleep? Probably the fawn nuzzling his cheek. And maybe also the hunger that was starting to dig a hole in the pit of his stomach. Setting the fawn down on the floor, he got up, went to the fridge, and poured himself half a glass of baby formula, just to see what it tasted like. It wasn't bad at first, but it left a too-sweet taste in his mouth.

Jeremy was heading to the sink when the clock caught his eye. No wonder he was starved. But where was McAdam? Probably burying the deer and cleaning out the pens. If so, Jeremy ought to be out there helping. Setting the fawn down in the bathroom beside a pot of water and a dish sprinkled with salt, he went out and headed for the enclosures.

But the buck, already growing cold and stiff, lay where it had fallen. A couple of squawking black turkey vultures were wheeling in the sky above it on wingspans almost as wide as a boy's outstretched arms. In the smaller pen, the dummy mother still lay in pieces amid the ruins of the rain shelter.

The truth hit Jeremy, making his skin tingle and sending a chill up his back. McAdam had gone after Stroud!

Jeremy crossed the field, looking for any sign of the men. His roaming eye picked out a dark mound down among the weeds and high grass. Was that McAdam? Jeremy called his name, but there was no answer. He broke into a run.

It wasn't McAdam who was lying there. It was Mitzi. Maybe this was just one of the ways she played tag, lying still until you came real close, then springing away from you.

But Jeremy didn't really believe this. He sensed already that something was wrong. And the closer he came to her, the more he began to dread what he would find.

"Mitzi," he called softly. "I don't like the game this way. Just jump up and run. Please, Mitzi, are you going to get up?"

He came all the way to her and she still didn't move. Jeremy knelt beside her, letting the fingers of both hands trail over her fur. His left hand touched something wet and sticky, and he turned the palm up.

It was blood.

Jeremy's entire face crumbled, while his chest filled with so much grief, it almost burst. He stood up, then dropped quickly to wipe the blood off on the grass as he wept. His one remaining hope was that she had died right away. He could not bear to think of Mitzi suffering as the buck had before McAdam shot it.

His thoughts went sharply back to McAdam. He must know about this by now. Even worse, he might have seen the killing.

And if he had . . .

The man could not have watched this happen and still be able to keep it together. Not McAdam, who couldn't see a difference between a person and a wild animal, especially one that he loved. McAdam would have gone out of his mind.

Jeremy knew that Stroud was crazy, too, but his was a different kind of craziness. Stroud was crazy like Ed. Craziness always worked for Ed. He not only *wanted* to be crazy, he was *proud* of it. He knew how to use being crazy to keep ahead of you, get what he wanted from you. Craziness was what made him control Mom. Craziness was what was going to give him the last drop of his revenge upon Jeremy.

And craziness was what Stroud was using now against McAdam.

The two men, Ed and Stroud, had almost melted together in Jeremy's mind by now. As Jeremy plunged into the woods, he thought about how people like them were so crammed full of anger and resentment, they refused to go down all by themselves. Oh, no. They had to drag everyone else with them.

But where was Stroud now? The only destination Jeremy could think of was the lodge. Recalling Stroud's directions, he kept going until he found the cliff. There he noticed a thin column of smoke, about half a mile away, where the sides of the gorge seemed to come together.

That way!

The powerful steel teeth made McAdam scream, but they also jolted him back to his senses. The spurts of pain that shot up his leg and through his body like flames were telling him to concentrate *now*. If he didn't, he'd be destroyed!

Crossing his free leg over the caught one, McAdam brushed away the leaves covering the trap and saw that it was the same one he'd tried to smash to pieces the day before.

McAdam gave a bitter grunt of appreciation for the cunning of his enemy. Luckily though, Stroud, who must have been working on the device half the night, hadn't managed to fix it entirely. The teeth that had bitten through the front of his boot and into his skin were still so bent that they hadn't crashed through the bone. The sharper ones in back, however, had buried themselves into the soft calf of his leg. McAdam could feel blood running between his toes and beginning to fill the boot. Already he was beginning to grow light-headed. How long would it be before numbness replaced the pain? Then he'd pass out. And then . . . death.

While there was still time to think and energy to act, McAdam studied the device. Two sets of springs stuck out from opposite sides of it. In order to release the trap those springs would have to be pressed down very hard at the same time. A trapper who'd caught a bear would simply finish the animal off, then use his hands. Well, McAdam had hands of his own. And if he could just manage to bend down very slowly and carefully . . .

As he started to squat, however, the pain grew worse, much worse. Bending was making the gash in his calf grow wider, making the back teeth bite more deeply. And the teeth in front, bent though they were, now pressed hard. He knew that if he did not let up immediately, his bones would snap.

McAdam thought about the best use of his shotgun. One shell remained. Would firing it bring help? There was no one living below. The gorge was nothing but a steep drop into a dried-out river bed. And the cliff · above him would muffle most of the sound. Who would hear it except Stroud himself? Jeremy was too far away. In fact, McAdam was thankful for that. It was unthinkable to put that boy in any more danger.

On the other hand, he could save the shell. And if he hadn't bled to death before Stroud came to gloat, there might be a chance to blow the man's head off.

But this thought only brought more weariness. Something else was flowing out of McAdam besides blood: the desire for revenge. For it was getting even that he had wanted, not justice. Justice had nothing to do with lashing out in blind violence because of the hurt. Wasn't that very same fury what had led him into this trap?

McAdam took the shotgun from his shoulder and gazed at the trap once more. Anything fired from this gun wouldn't be likely to make a clean hole. Was it possible to blow away one of the springs without taking his whole leg with it? He didn't see how. And then there would be the bits and pieces of metal rebounding everywhere.

It would be like shooting himself.

CHAPTER 12

Jeremy heard the shotgun blast echoing through the gorge. He had been keeping out of sight on a footpath about twenty feet into the trees. Now he threw aside all thought of his own safety. Rushing into the open, he raced along the rocky cliffside, shouting McAdam's name.

But his cries died out among the silent trees, leaving only the sound of his running feet. The two sides of the gorge were much closer together now. He must be near that little iron bridge Stroud had talked about, but his view was blocked by the steeply rising ground.

Jeremy scrambled uphill, grabbing bushes and finding footholds among roots. Suddenly, there was the bridge—and on the other side of it, the lodge itself. He caught his breath, then cupped a hand to his mouth.

"Stroud!"

Before he could repeat the shout, an engine started

up somewhere on the other side of the bridge. An all-terrain vehicle nosed out from a clump of trees, with Stroud behind the wheel. Giving the boy a friendly wave, he drove onto the bridge and stopped in the middle. Jeremy saw the rifle across his legs.

"You're just in time to take a ride with me," Stroud called. "I'm getting a few of these in shape for the club members. This baby here is gonna climb like a mountain goat."

"Where is he?" Jeremy bellowed.

"I ain't a mind reader, kid. Who are you taking about?"

"You know exactly who!"

Stroud's lips curled slowly into an amused grin. "Well, well, well. Now this is something. Are you telling me that Aaron McAdam is lost? That man who thinks he's lord of creation can't even find his own way on what he calls his own property. And you're coming to me to help you find him."

"Stroud, you're a crock! I'll kill you if you shot him!"

"You will, huh?"

"Yeah. I will!"

"Well, I didn't shoot him. Wouldn't shoot him. Don't intend to shoot him. You want to know why? Because I'm a hunter. Hunters know the difference between animals and people. It's your uncle who don't know that."

"Yeah, you are some hunter, all right. You fire into pens at helpless animals! You set traps that don't give them a chance. You murdered Mitzi!"

"Mitzi? I don't know a lady by that name."

"Aaron's bear!"

"Oh, *that* bear? She died, huh?"

"As if you didn't know!"

"No, I didn't know it till now, to tell the truth. But it couldn't be helped. She came at me. She was dangerous."

"If she came at you, it was just to *play*!"

"How would I know that?"

"Because you spy. And you killed her on *his* land!"

Stroud's eyes narrowed. "Well, that's *your* story. Mine is it didn't happen there. That bear started charging over this bridge. Now you can say it wanted to play, but I don't play with no bears. And from what I saw, that one would have been all over me if I hadn't shot it. But it turned and ran after I hit it. So I kept firing from here because a wounded animal is a menace. I would have chased the bear to make sure it was finished off if it wasn't for McAdam's getting that court to keep anybody from hunting on his property."

Stroud paused to reach down for a can of beer. He pulled the tab off and took a long drink. "Now as for somebody shooting into the pens," he continued, "this is the first I heard about it."

This guy is smarter than Ed, Jeremy fumed as he moved closer. He's got an answer for everything. He's done something to Aaron, and he'll get away with that, too.

Well, Jeremy wasn't going to stand for it. He'd had

enough! Almost without thinking, he reached back to the handle sticking out of the sheath on his belt.

Stroud was completely unafraid when he saw the blade lifting out. "Oh, you're going to come at me with that?"

His mistake was taking the time to laugh. Jeremy sprang so fast that the man had no time to react. One hundred ten pounds of crashing boy toppled him halfway off the vehicle. On top of him now with his knees digging into Stroud's chest, aware of nothing but his hatred, Jeremy swung the blade at the man's face.

Stroud ducked to the left just in time for the knife to go zinging by. Jeremy slashed at him crosswise, and Stroud ducked to the right, but almost too late. The knife passed through his close-cropped hair.

Stroud's hands grabbed the back of Jeremy's sweater, clutching wool, trying to wrench him off.

But Jeremy would not be stopped. He wasn't even thinking anymore, just striking back at everything that had ever made him feel helpless. With a cloth-tearing lurch, Jeremy pulled free, leaving Stroud defenseless. He brought up the knife once more, this time directly over the man's face.

Confronted with his own extinction, the doomed man neither begged nor whimpered. He exploded with laughter. "You wildcat! I like the way you go at it, kid. You're just like me!"

Jeremy flinched. And in that instant, the man acted. Powerful hands seized the boy's wrists and bent them back. Stroud's pressing thumb forced the knife hand to open. And as the blade dropped, a backward swipe of his forearm sent Jeremy flying to the deck of the bridge.

"Kid, you're a little criminal," Stroud said pleasantly, the rifle back in his hands. "You belong in jail, but I like you anyway. And since I'm the best tracker I know, I'm going to help you find your missing uncle."

Stroud stepped out of the ATV and waited until Jeremy got to his feet. "Now, why don't we use our heads first?" Stroud continued. "If you're so sure he was coming after me, how do you think he would do it?"

Jeremy said nothing.

"Want my opinion? I don't think he'd take the bridge. No, I think he'd probably have gone down to the lower ledge where he could cross over and sneak up on me from behind. But that's a tricky place, kid. If you lose your balance, you've had it. If McAdam dropped into the gorge, maybe that's what the shot was about. He bounced off one of the sides and his gun went off. Why don't we go and see?"

"He wouldn't fall off," Jeremy growled as they set out along the side of the gorge.

"Well, maybe you're right. Maybe he just stepped into that bear trap I tossed away. I thought it went all the way down, but I suppose it could have landed on that ledge."

Jeremy whirled around on him. "Landed! You put it there!"

"What? When it was all screwed up and broken like that? You've got to be kidding. It looked useless to me, so I got rid of it. 'Course it is possible that it might still kind of work. Anyway, we'll find out now. The ledge is just below there. Go take a look."

Jeremy rushed forward calling, "Aaron!" Then he saw him.

McAdam's damaged leg dangled over the side, the trap hanging loosely around it. One set of springs had been blown off by the shot, and he'd more or less managed to release the other set. But flying shards of metal and rock had torn through clothing and into his side and his arm. Blood streaked the back of his neck and the part of his face that was visible.

Dropping down beside the unconscious man, Jeremy pulled McAdam back from the edge. But that was all he could manage by himself. "Help me get him up there!" he shouted to Stroud.

Stroud made no move. And when the boy looked up at those narrowed eyes he saw at once what the man was thinking.

"Albert, you'd have to murder both of us," Jeremy said evenly.

Stroud was in no hurry to reply. He popped a cigarette into his mouth, lit it, and squatted by the edge of the cliff. "Now let's say I do just that, then shove you both over the side," he said at last. "What's my problem? Who's ever going to find your bodies after I rearrange some rocks down there?"

"Who? The folks who are going to come looking for us."

"Oh really? Well, remember when you called me a spy? Okay, I spied. McAdam don't have a family anymore. His wife moved out a long time ago and he don't get no visitors. And now let's take you. I got the feeling you're that missing kid I've been hearing about on the police radio, the one who ran away because his mother was arrested over at the market. That was on Friday, wasn't it? That's the day McAdam goes into town and does his shopping, I believe. Brings back his candy bars for the bear."

Jeremy glanced at the shotgun lying partway over the edge. Stroud wagged a finger and grinned. "I'm all over your mind, kid, but I don't think the gun is loaded. Tell you what, though. Just in case, kick it all the way off."

Jeremy hesitated.

"Watch it, kid. I've been good to you so far."

" 'Cause you like me, right?" Jeremy snapped through gritted teeth as he shoved the gun over.

"Sort of," agreed Stroud, with a troubled look. "So here we are. And now we come down to it, don't we?"

"What we come down to . . ." Jeremy took a deep breath ". . . is you don't kill us."

"Oh, really? Why's that?"

"First of all, because no matter what you say about how easy it'd be to get away with it, I don't think you like the idea of taking a chance."

Stroud frowned. "And what's the rest of it?"

"The rest is you ain't that type of guy, right? You know, a *criminal* like me . . . instead of a hunter like yourself."

"You got a mouth on you, kid."

"Yeah, I know. Any reason why you can't hear what my mouth is saying to you?"

"I'm listening."

Jeremy looked at Stroud. "What if you were the type of guy who got him to the hospital?"

"Then what?"

"Then this was an accident."

"Oh, you'd say that?"

"Yeah. If you didn't tell anyone I tried to put a knife through your throat."

"So you want to make a deal, huh?"

"Right. A deal. I don't need another gig in Juvie Hall. Besides, what happened to McAdam *was* an accident wasn't it?"

"Definitely. But what's he going to say about it?"

"I don't know. But here's what *I* say. The bear's dead and nobody can change that. But you're going to be *saving* this man's life now, right?"

"Why would I want to do that for him?"

"Because you either kill me, too—which you're not too happy about since I've never done anything to you—or you help the man. That's how it is. And you're even with him now, Albert, *more* than even! You just said yourself he was alone. That bear was his *family*!

Taking care of those animals was what made his life mean something. And look at him! Do you hate this guy even now?"

"Me?" Stroud grunted. "I don't give jack spit about him. But he's still in my face."

"Somebody will always be in your face."

"But not him."

"Then the law will be in your face."

"Maybe. Maybe not." Stroud looked off in the distance.

"And there's one thing more, Albert." Jeremy waited.

"What's that?"

"All of this ain't feeling so good anymore."

Stroud slowly finished his cigarette. "You're smart," he said at last.

"Yeah. I'm real smart."

"I'd do it, but I still don't know what *he's* gonna say."

"The boy," moaned a voice so weak that it could barely be heard, "speaks for me."

Having made his decision, Stroud moved swiftly. Bounding to the ledge, he boosted the wounded man on his back and set him down on the cliff above. "Get that boot off his foot, kid, so I can see the punctures."

Jeremy undid the laces and pulled. As soon as the boot came away in his hands a tide of blood poured out. But the gashes themselves had clotted over. Had they been flowing as freely as in the beginning, McAdam might already be dead.

As it was, he had lapsed into unconsciousness again, and they had to hurry. Lifting the man once again, Stroud half-ran, half-staggered across the bridge and up the slope to a battered old van that was parked on the other side of the hunting lodge.

They laid McAdam down on a mattress in the back of the van. Jeremy stayed with him while Stroud started the engine and began a wild ride down the mountain road which ran along the side of Devil's Gorge to the tiny village at the bottom. But no doctor had an office here, so Stroud raced through the village without stopping.

The ten miles to the outskirts of Medford disappeared in less than seven minutes. Just ahead now were two sets of traffic lights, both of them red. Stroud plowed right through them.

As he passed the second light, a sheriff's department car came jolting out of a deli after him. Stroud put the right turn signal on and pulled over to the shoulder of the road before the siren could start screaming. "No sense making them madder," he said. "Let me do the talking."

The same deputy who had quarreled with McAdam behind the feed store walked up to the driver's window with a hand on his holster. But when he saw who was at the wheel he relaxed. "What's going on there, Albert?" he asked. "Isn't it a little early in the day to be breaking the law?"

"Got Aaron McAdam in back. We're taking him to the hospital."

Tippet seemed amazed and leaned in to have a look. "You shoot him and change your mind?"

"Hell no. If I'd shot him, he'd be a trophy on my wall. Besides, it's out of season on wildlife preserves. Better let me get going."

The deputy stared at the young passenger. In his pocket was a grainy Xerox of a runaway's photograph. Jeremy began violently coughing into his hands.

"Who's the boy?"

"He's helping me. Maybe he needs a doctor, too. Here, kid." Stroud shoved a dirty handkerchief at Jeremy. Then he drummed his fingers impatiently on the wheel. "The man could die on us while I'm waiting."

The deputy shifted his glance to McAdam and frowned. "Want an escort?"

"No, I'm practically there. Just let me get going."

A couple of minutes later, the van slammed to a halt in front of the hospital. Stroud lifted McAdam out of the van while Jeremy raced inside for help. A nurse and an attendant pushing a stretcher took over in the emergency room, immediately wheeling McAdam through another door for treatment.

A clerk called Stroud over to her, and he began to give his version of the "accident."

McAdam, he said, had stepped into some old, half-buried trap. That took him by surprise, naturally. And it must have been such a shock that the shotgun he was carrying fell out of his hand. When it hit the ground it went off and caused the other injuries. When McAdam's nephew grew worried about him, he came to Stroud for help. By the time they found the man, he'd lost a lot of blood.

Stroud paused to glance over his shoulder. "Something more you want to tell her about it . . . *Jason?*"

Jeremy didn't answer. He had been standing by the swinging door, holding it partway open and looking inside.

"Hey, kid!"

"What?"

"I was just telling the nurse how it happened. You got anything to say about it?"

"No, nothing," he said quickly, his mind completely on something else. "Lady, I just saw the nurse come out of the room they put him in. But nobody else went inside."

"Please take a seat. I'm sure your uncle is being taken care of."

"Yeah? When my mom was in the hospital it was over an hour before a doctor even looked at her!"

"I'm sorry but I can't pay attention to two things at once. And right at this moment . . ." She reached for the phone, giving Stroud an apologetic look. "I hope you understand, sir, but by law *any* gunshot wounds have to be reported to the police. Someone will come and speak to you both about it."

Jeremy gave a start. If the police found out who he was, they'd yank him away in a flash and ship him down to the city. He couldn't let that happen, not when McAdam was hurt like this. And besides, the fawn needed him, too, especially now.

A shock ran through him. "Oh, my God," Jeremy exclaimed, and shot across the waiting room.

"Wait up, kid. What's happening?"

"The fawn! I never got to feed him! He's just a baby. He'll get very sick!"

As Jeremy pushed though the outside door, Stroud

started to follow. But the clerk called out, "Do not leave, sir. Please! He has to come back, too."

The man stopped. But the boy kept on going, streaking past the parked vehicles to the curving exit ramp and down into the streets of the town.

CHAPTER

Rushing to the edge of town, Jeremy stuck out his thumb. As a long string of vans and pickups whizzed by without stopping, his concern grew. The poor little fawn would be bleating by now and feeling awfully hungry. And if he didn't get fed soon enough, he could get very sick!

Finally, Jeremy caught a hitch on a Ford truck that had a gun rack behind the driver's seat . The young man at the wheel asked him whether he was cutting school tomorrow for the first day of the hunting season.

The word "tomorrow" rang in Jeremy's ears. All the rest of the killing was going to start *tomorrow*. And McAdam was in the hospital, unable to do a thing about it!

"Oh, I'll be there all right," said Jeremy, thinking about those monster firecrackers. His eyes turned bright with determination. "Not a chance in the world I'm gonna miss *that.*"

The driver let him out a mile short of the road that went up to the wildlife preserve. Jeremy dashed as far as the Devil's Gorge Store. Although breathing hard, he was ready to tackle the mountain when a delivery van backed out of the parking lot.

As it blocked his way, the painted words DAIRY PRODUCTS made Jeremy wonder about the amount of formula left in the refrigerator. Maybe if he made it real fast . . .

Hurrying inside he dashed to the dairy case. To make the formula he needed to blend milk with egg yolks. Grabbing what he needed, he galloped up to the register.

The woman there gazed right past him. She was listening to three old men in work clothes and caps. Seated over paper cups of coffee at the store's only table, they were recalling Thanksgiving dinners they'd had in the past.

"The best one I ever had," said one man, "was the day after I shot a wild turkey up on the mountain. I had just turned nine and I did it with just one shot out of a 22-caliber gun. Well, my mother didn't have the heart to tell me until years later that the turkey couldn't have fed even one of us, because it was all skin and bones. So she went out to the henhouse and killed the oldest layer, then threw it all in a pot and called it turkey fricassee!"

Jeremy stood at the counter waving one of the ten-dollar bills he had earned, tapping his feet. Finally, the woman took the bill. "Anything else?"

"No."

"You sure you didn't forget anything?"

"Yeah, I'm sure."

"Cheer up," she said, looking at him at last. "Life can't be *that* bad." When Jeremy frowned, she added with a smile, "And since you're my one millionth customer today, you win a prize. Have a candy bar. It's on the house."

Jeremy's gaze traveled across coconut bars, peppermints, and chocolate morsels, then came to a halt at the Tootsie Rolls. He felt a lump in his throat and his eyes misted over. "No, thanks," he muttered huskily. "I'm okay."

"Suit yourself," said the woman, making change. "But I've never met a boy who didn't grab candy when he had the chance. Where are you visiting from? New York?"

Jeremy nodded, starting to read the sign on the wall just behind her head.

"Who are you staying with?"

The sign said: "HUNTERS WELCOME. WE'LL CUT, FREEZE, AND WRAP YOUR DEER MEAT FOR ONE DOLLAR PER POUND."

"Up the mountain," Jeremy said.

The old men glanced at him. One of them lifted his bushy eyebrows. "With McAdam?"

Jeremy stiffened. "That's right," he shot back as if meeting a challenge.

"Tell him," the man went on, "to watch out for Albert Stroud. He's crazy."

"That's a fact," another man agreed. The conversation shifted to something else.

Free to go at last, Jeremy took his money and his bag of groceries and turned to the door.

Mitzi's head was mounted just above it. A corncob pipe had been shoved into her mouth, and she wore a tilted Smokey the Bear hat that make her look drunk.

Jeremy gagged. The groceries fell from his hand, landing in a splatter of milk and broken eggs. As he doubled over, gripping his stomach, the alarmed woman hurried out from behind the counter. "What's the matter?" she cried.

Jeremy didn't answer. He was coughing, throwing up. Before anyone could touch him, he raced out the door and ran headlong into the road. The storekeeper came out after him, the old men behind her. But if anybody was calling him, he couldn't hear it. *Wouldn't* hear it. He was already well on his way, not looking back, just running.

The fawn was bleating pitifully and there was a mess on the bathroom floor. But it was alive! Seeing the animal lifted Jeremy's spirits so much, he almost forgot about McAdam maybe dying in the hospital . . . and Mitzi lying out there in the field without her head.

The fawn was sleeping peacefully in his lap when Jeremy made his first call to the hospital. He'd been afraid of what he might hear, but it turned out he couldn't get any information at all. The woman who answered transferred him to another woman, who insisted that he put "some adult member of Mr. McAdam's family on the phone."

"Okay, okay. That's how you want it? Fine. My big brother's gonna be here any second! *He'll* call you."

Jeremy hung up and ran around trying to find something he could use to muffle his voice. Plastic wrap gave off a bad buzzing sound. Paper towels did nothing. At last he tried talking very low into a water glass. The voice that came out was deep and hollow like a foghorn. It sounded phony, but what else could he do?

The young man who answered the phone hesitated as if in confusion, then said "just a minute." He came back a moment later to say that the operation was over. Mr. McAdam's condition was listed as critical.

"Critical?" repeated Jeremy, so anxious that he forgot to disguise his voice. "What does *that* mean? Is he going to die?"

"I'm afraid that's all I can tell you."

"No, it isn't *all*!" he shouted. "We're talking about my . . . my *father*!"

There was another pause. "Hold on." The voice came back, sounding a bit friendlier. "This is just between us, all right?"

"Yeah."

"The head nurse said he seems to be coming out of it."

"Out of what? Was he in a *coma* or something?"

There was another pause. "Do you know about shock?"

"Not too much," Jeremy admitted.

"Well, I'm no doctor or nurse, and frankly I'm not all that clear about this sort of thing myself. How old is your dad?"

"I don't know. He's pretty old."

"You don't *know*?"

"He was in the war."

"Which war?"

"I'm . . . I'm not sure."

"Desert Storm? Vietnam? Korea? Stop me if I'm getting warm." There was a short silence, and Jeremy knew the guy was on to him. "The man isn't your dad, is he?"

"I'm his friend, okay? He's helping me! I work for him! Look, he's got a little animal up here I'm taking care of for him! Can you stop giving me such a hard time? I gotta know how he is!"

"I can just tell you that he's holding his own. There are other calls waiting. I have to go."

Jeremy slammed the phone down. The call was a waste of time, leaving him too agitated to stay there with the fawn and do nothing. Especially when Mitzi was lying out there without a head!

I'm going to bury her.

Leaving the fawn behind, Jeremy rushed out to the feed barn, pulled McAdam's shovel from the little crawl space, and went into the field.

Mitzi had flies around her body now—but she still had her *head!* He'd been wrong about the one he'd seen at the general store. Maybe it was because that head had been made to look stupid that he got so upset. That the bear's whole life came down to something to laugh at!

Yeah, but killing Mitzi was *also* somebody's idea of a joke. Albert Stroud's. Only Jeremy didn't want to think about that now. There was a lot of work ahead, digging into the hard, rocky ground.

It was dark before Jeremy had dug even a shallow grave. But his blistered hands were bleeding in spots, and he wanted to get back to the telephone and the fawn.

Using all the strength he could find, he shoved Mitzi into her final resting place and started covering her. With the coming of evening, the air had grown breezy and cold. Until now the hard work had kept Jeremy warm. But with his clothes damp from sweat and nothing to do but find the right words to say over her body, a chill was entering his bones. What could he say?

Maybe there wasn't any prayer that was right. "We both liked her a lot," was all Jeremy could think of before he turned away from the graveside. But then he stopped, looked back over his shoulder for a moment, and lifted his eyes to the first stars of the oncoming night.

"She didn't deserve this, God! Just like Aaron didn't deserve to be hurt. Just like my mom doesn't deserve it. Just like lots of animals and people don't deserve what's happening to them all the time. So this thing about justice and fairness and all that—you want to show me where it is? Now that's something I'm really waiting for!"

CHAPTER

15

Jeremy brought the box of firecrackers from McAdam's truck into the house, and rolled three dozen of them out on the kitchen table. Those suckers were *big!* Not at all like the ones kids threw at your feet on the Fourth of July, then ran away laughing. These were going to go off like bombs!

Where were the best places to explode these tomorrow in order to wake up the forest? For starters, along the cliff where the echo would carry the warning to as many animals as possible on both sides of the gorge. After that, wherever he could find a footpath or a place the hunters might go.

But Jeremy would have to do all of this before the sun came up. He set the clock for four-thirty. That way he'd have time to feed the fawn before he left.

Jeremy brought the clock down from its perch on the refrigerator and carried it out of the kitchen. He might as well get to bed now, especially since there was no fire and he felt too tired to scrounge up a meal. The fawn had been watching his every movement. Now it followed him to the sleeping bag and sank down beside him, burying its nose in the sweet-smelling brush Jeremy had placed on the floor.

The hours ticked away, but Jeremy could not really rest. At last he fell into a doze. But he was on his feet even before the clock began to jangle.

Jeremy searched around until he found a flashlight and matches, then swept the firecrackers into a shopping bag and hurried out. But he didn't even need the flashlight out in the open. Although there was no moon, a vast umbrella of stars sparkled in the cool morning air. And when Jeremy went among the trees on the other side of the field, he quickly grew used to the darkness. He didn't feel a bit tired as he made his way to the edge of the gorge. In fact he felt very much alive as he hurried along the cliff, then up the hill that led to the metal bridge.

His eyes scanned the hunting lodge. The big building was dark, but there were many parked vehicles crowded near it. Obviously, some of the members had spent the night there so they could get a quick start in the morning. He'd give them a quick start, all right!

Dropping to his hands and knees, Jeremy crept to the center of the bridge and set down the first firecracker. Then he crawled to the edge, leaned over the side, and placed another one on a beam just underneath the surface of the span. He lit the fuse of this one first, then lit the firecracker on top of the bridge. Then he sprang to his feet and ran for it.

He'd barely made it to the trees when the firecracker on the beam exploded. The whole bridge rattled like a kettledrum. Then the second one went off. Together, they made pounding waves of sound that felt like an earthquake. Lights went on all over the lodge. Jeremy stayed around just long enough to see men piling out the front door in their thermals, cursing and holding their ears.

Now for the rest of it! Jeremy hurried to light other fuses deep inside the wooded areas surrounding the field. When he finished there, he doubled back past the farmhouse, went through the grove, and began climbing. He'd saved the last six firecrackers for the spot just above the cave where McAdam hoped his beloved bear would give birth to her cubs. He bunched these firecrackers together, like the candles of a birthday cake, on the high summit overlooking the gorge and the valley below. When they went off, it was like a final farewell to Mitzi.

The telephone was ringing as he neared the cabin. Jeremy broke into a run. But before he could get to the door, he heard someone inside pick up the receiver and say, "No, you got the right number."

It was Stroud!

Was the guy drunk and crazy again? Jeremy stopped to listen.

"You *know* who I am, McAdam. And I'm looking for

him, too. He's been out since about five setting off a bunch of M-80 simulated land mines to scare away the deer. Won't change anything and it was a real dumb thing to do, so I guess he got the idea from you."

Silence.

"Why am I looking? To make sure nobody creams him for it. Also, my guess is you never had enough sense to cut off some candlewicks and tie them on to make the fuses on those damn things longer. I want to see if the kid blew off any part of himself. That way I can take him to the hospital, too, on my way out of here. I figure I owe it to him for keeping me from letting you die. Not that I give a damn about you, you understand. But unless I'm out of my head, I have to be in a war to go and kill any man."

Quietly, Jeremy opened the door. But he was wrong if he didn't expect Stroud to be aware of it.

"McAdam, he just came in. Looks like he's still got both his eyes and—hold up your hands, kid—all his fingers, too. So that's it. You can talk to him now. I'm gone. What?"

Jeremy stepped forward to take the phone, but Stroud was still talking. "Where to?" he repeated. "What do you care? Anywhere! I just can't stand looking over a bridge at the land that three hundred years of my family are buried under."

Stroud paused. Then a voice that almost belonged to a different person came out of him. "It's what it does to me inside. I just don't like how it's changed me . . . What?

. . . Wait, wait. Back up and say that again. Maybe I didn't get what you . . ."

Jeremy watched Stroud with growing excitement. Something big was happening here!

"Do I want to *buy* some of the land? I don't understand."

Stroud listened intently. But when he spoke, the gruffness was back in his voice. "Lemme get this straight. I can have the orchard and the old house and half the field, but the deed's gonna say I can't ever hunt on it? This is crazy, McAdam! If that land is going to be mine, then I can do anything I want to on it . . . What? What are you calling me? Yeah, well, I ain't the only one who's *pigheaded* around here. But we're talking, all right? That's a start. When you get out, we'll talk some more."

Jeremy watched him grow silent and hold back a sigh. "Yeah, yeah, yeah," Stroud grunted. "Well, who knows— anything is possible. Now about this kid here and the stuff he's been pulling . . ."

Stroud turned to Jeremy, his rugged face showing the barest trace of a smile. "McAdam says he doesn't want to keep lying to your mother about you being safe up here."

"Keep lying?"

Stroud, listening again, held up his hand. "He says he got the number from the deputy and he called her. Wait a minute. She's going to be calling you to see if you want to stick out the rest of the school year up here."

"Are you going to let me talk to him?" Jeremy barely noticed the pat on his shoulder as he tore the phone away from Stroud. "Aaron, when are you getting out of there?"

McAdam sounded weak and tired. "That I don't know, son. At this point I have to keep sneaking out of my room just to get to the phone. So let me speak quickly before some nurse discovers me hobbling around and drags me off. If you hear that I'm in Intensive Care and can't see anyone for awhile, that's just the usual hospital nonsense. I'm going to be all right. So does this count as my breaking a promise not to butt in between you and your mom?"

"Yes. But . . . but I'm glad you did."

"Well, that's a relief. Now, no more setting off firecrackers, Jeremy."

"They're all gone. It was great!"

"How's the fawn?"

"He's great, too. And I buried Mitzi. I didn't do the buck yet, but—"

"I'd stay away from him, Jeremy. The body could be contaminated by now. Better call the vet."

"Aaron, when are you coming back?"

McAdam chuckled. "Asking me that a second time won't make it any sooner. On the other hand, maybe it will. You're giving me plenty of reason for wanting to hurry back."

Stroud left, and for the next half hour, Jeremy barely moved from the phone. What was going on? Why wasn't Mom calling? Had she changed her mind? Was Ed beating her?

When the phone finally jangled, he snapped it up. "Mom?"

"You must hate me for being so weak!" She was sobbing.

"No, Mom!"

"Well, I am weak. I know that. I wish it was different, Jeremy. And maybe it will be. But right now, I just don't know how to be different. Darling, Ed isn't a bad man."

"I don't want to talk about him!"

"All right. I understand. That man who's your friend up there, you do know I spoke to him, right?"

"Yes."

"He sounds very nice. But I haven't met him. And I would feel better if—"

"So why don't you come up and see him, Mom? That would be terrific."

"Yes, darling, just as soon as Ed—"

"No, Mom! I want you to come by yourself."

"I will, darling. I will. I just need . . ." Her voice trailed off. "Tell me about Mr. McAdam. Are you sure that he isn't—well, you know—isn't *funny* in some way?"

"Mom, he's not!"

"Just the same, I'm going to ask the social worker from Child Protective Services—you know, the one who always came to the shelter—to visit you right away and find out everything she can about him."

"Mom, I wish you wouldn't."

"I'm your mother! And I *will* do it. Even Mr. McAdam agreed with me that I should! So if you want me to let you stay at all—"

"Yes, I do!"

"And . . . and . . . you are not to think of yourself as living in some foster home, do you understand that?"

"Mom—"

"Jeremy, I lived in foster homes. So did Ed. And I won't have you doing that! This is just temporary, a long visit. It gives me a chance to get certain things straight in my own head. Jeremy, I know I haven't always been a good mother to you. But I've been so mixed up! And a person doesn't get stronger all at once, darling. Even at my age a person isn't always all grown up, you see?"

"Yeah."

"Don't *yeah* me."

"Mom, I understand."

"No, you don't. You think I've let you down. And I guess I have. So you went and found somebody, all on your own, who is like a father to you. But he could just as easily have been a terrible person! Still, you already have faith in him. And . . . and what I'd like you to do is . . . to have some faith in me, too. I'd like you to believe that your mother *can* get stronger."

"Mom, I do believe you can. It's just that—"

"Let's not talk about your objections! I know what your objections are. Some things take awhile . . . and . . ."

Jeremy thought he heard a sob. "Mom, don't cry," he begged her.

"Mr. McAdam," she said in a tiny voice, "told me you're learning about animals."

"Yeah, I am."

"Well, that's very nice and—"

"Mom, will you stop crying?"

"I can't help it. I feel like I'm losing my son!"

"But you're *not* losing me! I'm just here for a while
. . . until, you know . . ."

There was a long pause. "You're sure you still love
me?" his mother asked at last.

"Yes!"

"And you forgive me?"

He didn't answer.

"Jeremy?"

"I'm still pretty mad," he said at last.

"Mad at me?" She sounded like a small child.

No, he told himself. At the *moon.*

"But couldn't you get over it?"

"I think so, yeah. Yes. Look, you don't have to worry
about that now, okay?" This was getting more painful.
"Mom, I gotta go."

"Darling, I love you so much."

"I know that, Mom. I love you, too."

So much had been happening to Jeremy that he felt
as if he was in some kind of haze. He needed to do
something to break free of it. Only he just wasn't sure
what.

When he went to get a glass of milk for himself, the
nearly empty refrigerator provided an answer. But if he
walked down to the general store now, he'd have to face

the music for leaving all those broken eggs on the floor, not to mention barfing on them! Well, he'd been thinking about apologizing for that, anyway. Might as well get it over with.

But the fawn began to bleat the moment he tried to leave it in the pen. So, Jeremy made a shoulder sling out of his sweater and tucked the fawn inside. Then they set off together.

The long hike down to the store was relaxing. The weight he'd felt while he talked to his mom was lifting off his chest at last. He could imagine calling her back later today. Well, maybe tomorrow.

And McAdam was really going to get better. And they were going to live here together and do all kinds of saving the animals stuff.

Jeremy took a deep, free breath.

He thought of Stroud, and how McAdam had given the man a reason to let go of all that hating and blaming. It made Jeremy begin to feel better himself. By the time he reached the bottom and started walking along flat ground toward the store, Jeremy was almost glowing.

But then he saw the traffic going by on the main road—a long line of cars and vans and pickups. It was only the beginning of the afternoon on the first day of hunting season, yet almost every car had a dead deer tied to the top or back of it.

Jeremy carried his fawn into the store, feeling more like a fugitive than a customer. He kept his eyes down so he wouldn't have to see the bear's head over the inside of the door. Going quickly to the dairy case and then to the shelves, he took his purchases to the counter and pulled out his money.

The cashier stared at him.

"Sorry for the mess I made," Jeremy muttered, thrusting the bill at her.

"That's funny. I don't remember any mess," said the woman. "I like your fawn. He's cute."

"Thanks."

Jeremy heard chairs scraping behind him. An old man said, "They're *all* cute. Only you don't do them any favors by taming them. You can't keep a deer like you would a dog. Treating them that way just sets them up for the next hunt."

"Never mind him," said the woman with a sigh. "We all do what we have to do. Here's your change."

"Thanks."

"You won't see what's different around here if you don't look around," said the woman as Jeremy turned away to the door with his eyes still on the floor. "I've redecorated."

Cautiously, he lifted his gaze. The tilted hat was gone. And so was the corncob pipe. And the head that had looked so much like Mitzi's—that was gone, too.

"That dustcatcher has been around long enough," said the woman. "But tell me something before you go. This being almost Thanksgiving and all, is it against your beliefs to eat a real nice turkey salad sandwich?"

She was taking one out of a case as Jeremy turned

around. Turkey? He'd always loved turkey. Confusion spread through him as he recalled that McAdam had served him bacon for breakfast—and that McAdam's boots were made of leather. There was a lot he'd have to talk over with his friend. "I . . . uh . . . I'm not . . ."

It made him feel stupid to be floundering around like this. He took a deep breath and said, "That offer of a prize for being your one millionth customer—is it still on?"

"Sure is."

Once again, Jeremy's glance passed over the chocolate bars and the peppermints. Then his fingers closed gratefully around the Tootsie Rolls.